A
Pattern
of
Shades

A Pattern of Shades

Wendy Dodds

Press

Published by 99% Press,
an imprint of Lasavia Publishing Ltd.
Auckland, New Zealand
www.lasaviapublishing.com

ISBN: 978-1-99-115194-0

Dedicated to Aotea Great Barrier Island

Acknowledgements

I wrote this Novel in 2010, five years after I returned to the mainland. It was originally written as a thesis for a Master of Creative Writing, capturing my musings on light and shade, and inspired by the events of 1984. I would like to acknowledge the guidance of my tutor Stuart Hoar.

I wish to acknowledge the work of Richard Wilhelm whose translation of the *I Ching*, (secondary translation from German by Cary F. Baynes) was my guide through the tumultuous Barrier years and provides structure to the book. I also drew on Fritjof Capra's *The Tao of Physics*. The quotation 'The map is not the territory,' comes from Alfred Korzybski's *Science and Sanity*.

My thanks to my family who have always supported me in my creative endeavours. Thanks also to the few close friends who read the second draft of the book. It, however, would still be languishing in a dusty box beneath my bed had Rosario Benoit not asked to read it again in 2019. Without her help and that of my good friend, Gael Johnson, it would never have come to the attention of the people at Lasavia Publishing: Michael Johnson, Rowan Sylva and Daniela Gast. I am grateful for Rowan and Daniela's gentle encouragement and for the work involved in publishing this novel.

Lastly I would like to thank Gael Johnson, Monique Von Ditzhuyzen, Jel Davenport, Fenella Christian, Phil Anderson and our projectionist, Peter Edmonds. Without their enthusiasm the song would never have been performed, and thus the book would never have been written.

Historical Note

When a heavily drunk Robert Muldoon announced that a snap election would be held on the 14th of July 1984, there was a lot of excitement. Change was in the air and we had hope for the future. New Zealand would go nuclear-free, the rights of women, Māori and homosexual people would be recognized, and a new era of environmental stewardship would begin. On Great Barrier Island, Fenella, who ran the General Store in Tryphena, organised a ball to be held at the hall on the election night. A group of us got together to perform a song that I thought up in the middle of the night. It was a heady time but afterwards the memory became buried under the struggles and unforeseen consequences of that election. Though inspired by these events and infused with the spirit of the time, *A Pattern of Shades* is a fictional work and the characters, events and places it depicts are literary creations.

Contents

Dramatis Personae

Mothers

Mouse: mother of **Tracey** and **Janey**, from Fissure Bay

Flash Kate: mother of **Thad** and **Melissa**, from Wairua

Big Lou: mother of **Ben**, **Nick** and **Gabe**, from Wairua

Patsy Dervish: mother of **Melissa**, from Wairua

Lizzie: mother of **Sam** (Samantha), shop owner

Fathers

Eddie: father of **Tracey** and **Janey**, partner of **Angel** and father of **Jesse**, from Fissure Bay

Pete: father of **Marama** and **Melissa**, from Wairua

Tom: father of **Ben**, **Nick** and **Gabe**, absent, from Wairua

Paul: father of **Sam**, partner of **Lizzie**

Others

Aussie Joe, from Wairua

Belle: **Patsy Dervish's** sister, lives in Ponsonby

Dutchie: lives on lifestyle block neighbouring Wairua

Horse Fly: ex-jockey, from Wairua

McLarens: **Dutchie's** neighbours with whom he is feuding

Mary-Anne: **Pete's** sister, lives on Waiheke

Old Tom: old man who lives alone by the wharf

Richie: visiting American

Reuben: friend of **Paul**, lives out beyond the wharf

Rose: runs the Post Office

Trev: from Fissure Bay

Difficulty in the Beginning

It's a Saturday morning in the depths of July and I'm sitting in a patch of sunlight outside the boatshed enjoying a C and J breakfast – coffee and joint that is – while the dragons in my mind squabble over how I should spend my free weekend.

Blithe Spirit's all for dancing over the sands ... *to the club ... maybe even a man ... some sex ... now that would be nice ... while the girls are away and you have the boatshed to yourself.*

Once you've done some housework, Stern Discipline trumpets. *Look at that washing! It's been soaking there for five days now.* The washing's fetid stench mingles with the wrackish tang of seaweed left by the storm. *And look at all that seaweed the storm's blown up!* he continues. *The garden could do with that; start building up some beds for spring.*

Why be out from under the covers at all? High Anxiety whines. *There's no need.*

Except that's where I've been for most of the last five days, hiding from the rain and the disorder that's been growing around me like fungus around a leak.

Over my right shoulder, Harshly Critical begins harping on about my many flaws and the impossibility of me ever finding love again.

Around me yawns the lonely void.

Eddie called in yesterday, quite out of the blue, coming in with his usual swagger, not even waiting for me to scramble down from the loft and look as if I hadn't been hiding under the covers since the children left for school. He threw his oilskin on to one of the aluminium drums that serve us as both food bins and seats and glanced around at the jumble of toys, clothes, books and dirty dishes that filled every empty space in the boatshed.

"This place's freezing," he commented. "You should line it ... just a few sheets of gib'd warm it up a bit."

Even so I was glad to see him. In the two months since we moved out of Fissure Bay, just after Easter, we've only had an occasional glimpse of him. Every morning Janey wonders aloud over breakfast if Daddy will come today. Tracey never answers but I can tell by the determined rhythm she spoons up her porridge with that she feels it too.

He's not a big man, is Eddie, but his restless energy fills up whatever space he's in. I watched him surreptitiously while I filled the kettle, turned on the gas bottle and lit the gas. He had cleared a space amongst the clutter of breakfast dishes on the table and was rolling a joint. Rust-coloured tendrils poked out from beneath his rolled-up balaclava and mingled with the bristles on his face. He'd obviously given up shaving now that Angel isn't there to keep him in line, but I didn't say anything. He never liked me commenting on his appearance.

"And how's Angel?" I asked dutifully, keeping my eyes on the coffee I was spooning into the mugs to keep my jealousy from escaping.

"She's good. I'm heading over there now. It's Jesse's birthday so I thought I'd take the girls over for the weekend. If you give us some clothes for them I can pick them up from school."

I'm huddled in my Swanni, keeping very still on the beer crate so as not to disturb the warm pod of air around me.

Stern Discipline pronounces it a good thing that Jesse's first birthday had completely slipped my mind – *Creating Some Distance. Getting On With Your Life.*

Maybe you should go over there, show you care. High Anxiety worries before the fear of socializing overcomes her.

I'll bet Angel won't be overjoyed having your girls around, sneers Harshly Critical. *You'd realise that if you weren't so gullible.*

But at least he's taken them, chimes in Blithe Spirit. *They'll be rapt to be spending time with their daddy and their little brother. And now you've got the whole weekend to run wild in.*

I take a hard drag on the joint, blasting out the neural pathways.

This morning I woke up happy. A song came into my head. It came out of the silence that wrapped itself around our little shed when the rain stopped in the early hours. I struggled up through a deep sludge of sleep to light a candle and scribble it down so that it remained as a backbeat to my dreams. I sing it aloud now in the growing warmth of the morning. Blessed, blessed indeed to have been sent such a gift from God.

All around there's the steady plink, plink of trees shedding their excess water, swelling as the load lightens, twisting and stretching their leaves towards the rising sun. Out in the Hauraki Gulf the white caps are still romping over one another but it's calmer here on shore. Gulls are preening themselves down on the shoreline where the dirty, khaki-coloured sea, swollen with fresh water and bush litter, slaps against the boat ramp. The sound echoes off the cliffs surrounding the bay.

Paul's boat's anchored just off the point again. I watch his spare outline messing about with lines and bait. Through another draw on the joint Blithe Spirit weaves a wonderful tale of he and I, our coming together, our doing it, our intimate conversations long into the night, I whispering to him all my hopes and dreams ...

Married! thunders Stern Discipline.

Then Harshly Critical begins his usual rant, while High Anxiety whimpers and moans.

I take a last drag on the joint and focus on the shifting patterns of light and shade cast by the pohutukawa tree down on the beach. For just a brief moment my mind is quiet and it seems like the dragons' cacophony has been silenced.

But Blithe Spirit can't shut up. *You're getting it now!* she crows.

Then Harshly Critical's bellow reverberates through the recesses of my mind. *That's a thought! You're still thinking. You can't shut us out!*

Sometimes I wish I could take off my head and store it in the rafters where I put my dope tin when I'm trying to give up.

Down on the beach a bark sets off a shrill yelling of gulls. They wheel and dive above a muttish black dog while she leaps and yaps. They play this game, Lilith and the gulls. On days when the wind's rising and the storm clouds pile up on the horizon, the gulls circle her, jeering with harsh cries, while she springs up to snap at their stick legs dangling just out of reach. Then on quiet days like this, when they're resting on the shore, she tears out unannounced, and they rise in a swarm to taunt and scream.

"Hi, Mouse." A willowy boy with a gap-toothed smile and a mop of corn-coloured curls slides out of the flax bushes flanking the track that leads up to the road.

"Thad." I straighten up and smile at him. I quite like Thad, even though he's too stroppy for his own good. Flash Kate's too soft with him in my opinion. Of course, I only have girls so maybe it's not for me to say.

"Mum wonders, could you come and give us a push. We want to go to the shop coz she's out of smokes, but the battery's flat 'cause she was playing tapes last night. She said maybe you'd like to come for the ride?"

I scan the bay. My eyes come to rest on Paul.

Best stay in bed where it's safe, murmurs High Anxiety. *What if he comes ashore while you're out and you miss him?*

He's not going to do that! Harshly Critical spits out.

The first time I ever talked to Paul was at Flash Kate's birthday party last month. I had been inclined to hide away in the boat-shed but the girls were keen to go and Kate was quite insistent, surprising seeing as she'd been avoiding me ever since we moved in.

The A-frame bulged with raucous chat and laughter but nobody spoke to me. I edged as far into a corner as the slope of the roof would allow and watched Angel telling Flash Kate some sordid tale. Kate listened intently and was obviously avoiding my eye so I slipped through the ranch sliders to the solitude of the deck. The wind was herding the clouds across the sky. I was absorbed in the movement of their shadows across the white-flecked sea when someone coughed behind me.

Paul unfolded himself from a chair against the wall and came to stand beside me. He's very tall and wears his hair in a ponytail that would make his long face look austere were it not for the luxuriant moustache that flows down either side of his mouth. I'd never really spoken to him before. Usually he keeps to himself and lets his wife, Lizzie, do all the talking. I felt kind of sheltered by him in a comforting way.

I started babbling on about how the shadows were moving and how that reminded me of the *I Ching*, which uses broken and unbroken lines to represent light and shade, all the time expecting him to dismiss the *I Ching* as superstitious nonsense. Surprisingly he listened intently. Then he told me about a book he was reading called *The Tao of Physics*, which was about the parallels between modern physics and Eastern mysticism. He offered to lend it to me when he'd finished it.

Just then Lizzie joined us and did that thing women do when they think you've been talking to their man too long. She draped herself around him and pretended to take a great interest in what we were talking about, fixing me with her eyes so that I ended up addressing everything I said to her. Eventually he went back inside and started talking to that guy, Reuben, who's helping him build their house. A few days later he dropped the book off and now he's often fishing off our point, so maybe ...

Only a desperate woman would stay in all day waiting for the impossible! jeers Harshly Critical.

You can't leave that washing another day, warns Stern Discipline.

Ah come on, whines Blithe Spirit. *It'll be fun.*

I sigh, rise out of the warm space I've cultivated around me and prepare to go – purse, gumboots, close door, ready.

"Hey, Lilith," yells Thad. "Come here, you dumb mutt!"

Lilith raises her head, sniffing the air. Then she tears up the beach, thrusting herself ahead of Thad to lead the way up through the flax and scrubby manuka to the A-frame on the other side of the gully.

When the present owners bought this land they lived in the boat-shed while they built the A-frame. After they moved in he found himself at a loose end so they returned to lucrative jobs in town and now they only come out over the silly season. Kate gave me their number to call when living over in Fissure Bay with Eddie and Angel had become too painful for me.

Of course, Angel's moved out now too – into a bach over on the other coast by the surf club. Maybe I should've stayed, except, well, correspondence school was causing a major rift between Tracey and I. She needed to go to school and Janey also started soon after we moved here ... probably it's for the best ... a first step out of the void I'm submerged in.

Out on the road, Kate's drumming an impatient tattoo on the roof of her brown A40. Thad's three-year-old sister Melissa chatters away to her from the back seat. Kate has all the poise of the Three Graces but she's all flat planes and sharp angles, rather like the cliffs beneath us. Her nose juts sharply upward, as if she's never got over being a vicar's daughter and somehow superior to all the country girls she went to school with. Tangled, blonde curls hang around her shoulders, trapped beneath the woolly hat – a Fair Isle pattern in bright pink, lime green and black – that Big Lou knitted for her birthday. The first two fingers of her left hand are brown from all the smoking that's been going on.

Cigarette smokers really are the worst addicts of all. In Fissure Bay – where it's a two-hour walk to the road before you even think about where you're really headed – they scrabble about in the litter beneath the wood-stove looking for butts when they've run out.

And what will you do when your dope runs out? asks Harshly Critical snidely.

High Anxiety flutters about in my stomach at the mere mention of my diminishing stash.

"How's it, Kate? Need a push?" I'm feigning casual confidence as I step up to the back bumper.

"Jeez, it's not easy, is it? Battery's flat again. Actually it's stuffed." Her well-rounded vowels float through the air like a wisp of smoke. "Pete's bringing me one back from town, whenever that is. How long does it take to paint a bathroom?" she asks of the morning as she lowers herself into the car.

I put my back against the rear bumper and push with my legs, rocking it back and forth a couple of times with Thad pushing manfully beside me. Soon it's on a roll. We run behind it, pushing it down the short slope before the road winds up and around again. Kate does the necessary tricky manoeuvres on the pedals.

Old Gert jumps a couple of times and coughs a bit. There'll be no second chances. I could end up looking after Kate's kids while she walks to the shop to satisfy her addiction. But good ole Gert's coming to the party. Flash Kate revs the motor hard and then settles it down to a steady throb while Thad and I rush to get in. The front passenger door's tied shut with drift rope but I've got pretty adept now at climbing through the window.

We chug off up the hill in silence.

You should say something, Stern Discipline instructs me.

"Pete's been gone a while now," I venture.

Pete is Melissa's dad, a sailor more in love with his catamaran than with the mothers of his kids. They are part of the Wairua crowd, one of the first land companies to set up on the island. Ever since Kate moved down to the A-frame she's been trying to lure him away to play happy families but it's not really working. He's always finding more exciting games to play elsewhere. He's been over on Waiheke painting his sister's bathroom for weeks now.

Kate's thin lips are a hard line across her face. The kids break into a fight in the back seat, and she yells at them.

No, not Pete, whispers High Anxiety. *She's tense with no tobacco. Don't incite her.*

"And when's Patsy coming back?" I ask once the children have been quelled.

Kate's long fingers are tightening on the steering wheel: her knuckles are white and bony.

"She was due back yesterday," she snaps, "but of course the boat didn't come because of the storm, did it! You really do ask stupid questions at times, Mouse!"

Yeah, well not that, snarls Harshly Critical.

Patsy Dervish is another of the Wairua folk but she lives down behind the shop now. Her daughter, Marama, is Pete's older daughter. Patsy hitched a ride with him when he sailed away to Waiheke and is still not back either. Big Lou's come down from Wairua to take care of Marama while she's gone.

A chill spreads throughout the car, even silencing the kids and the dog in the back seat. We travel on. Only the burr of the motor and the various rattles fill the silence.

High Anxiety shifts uneasily. *You've started out all wrong,* she twitters. *You'll have to walk back around the rocks as soon as you get to the shop.*

We drop down and follow the sea wall around the last corner. Flash Kate swings the car around and drives up towards the school a little way so she can get a good run when it comes time to leave. Even before the car comes to a standstill, Thad and Lilith are jostling to be the first to join Big Lou's three boys and Marama down on the beach.

"Thad, Thad, wait for me-e-e." Melissa's shrill gull cry rips through the silence as she toddles after him over the rough stones.

The dragons are clamouring for attention.

Stern Discipline reminds me that it's still three days to benefit day. *Take Care of the Pennies and the Pounds Will Take Care of Themselves,* he warns.

Meanwhile High Anxiety is doing macramé with my entrails. *Oh my God, people will know you're stoned. Keep hidden, keep hidden.*

Yeah, and if you can manage to keep your head down and mouth shut you might not make a fool of yourself, Harshly Critical murmurs.

But Blithe Spirit is singing the song again. I stride in time with the beat as I follow Flash Kate down to the shop where Big Lou's standing in a patch of sunlight debating with Old Tom whether Lizzie's even going to open today.

"It nearly eleven," she's reasoning, " ... and the boat didn't come in yesterday so there's no petrol." A large sign hanging on the petrol pump says just that. She gives us a quick smile but Old Tom's too busy chewing over the problem to notice us. He reckons that of course the shop will open because what about the Saturday paper and people wanting alcohol for the weekend?

"Or tobacco," puts in Kate. She turns slightly to cut off Old Tom, who has a tendency to go on.

"Any word from Pete?" she asks Big Lou.

Big Lou's scanning the horizon across the top of Old Tom's head while she chooses her words.

She's trying to tell Kate something she doesn't want you to know about, whispers High Anxiety.

Yeah, because you can't be trusted with gossip, observes Harshly Critical.

"Patsy called yesterday from Ponsonby," Lou answers at last. "Pete's still on Waiheke. She doesn't know when he's coming back." She swishes some water out of a small puddle with her gumboot. "She was going to be on the boat but ... as you know ... so she'll probably be on the Sea Bee tomorrow."

"Where're your kids, Mouse?" she asks me.

Their eyes fall on me like globules of hot fat. My fists are balled in the pockets of my Swanni keeping the dragons leashed.

"Ah, it's Jesse's birthday," I answer. "Eddie's taken them over to Angel's for the weekend."

"Re-e-ally? One already?" She's about to ask something else but Kate bursts out in a frustrated rave.

"Why doesn't Paul come and open the shop," she rants, "instead of fishing out our bay?"

"Ah, well," says Old Tom gently, "you can't keep a good man from his fishing. Lizzy'll be picking up the papers. Probably waiting for the airstrip to dry out so the plane can land."

Sensing a receptive audience, he launches into a tirade about the latest petition to get reticulated power to the island but really he's preaching to the converted. We're all waiting for alternative energy to become cheap enough for us to generate our own power without recourse to The Man. We see it as a variation on 'Power to the People'.

"They'll never get the cable across the channel," he drones. The pom-pom on top of his woolly hat bounces up and down as he emphasises his points with nods of his head. "And even if they do, it'll cost an arm and a leg. You see if it doesn't."

Lizzie's transit van swishes around to park by the generator shed beside the shop. Her daughter Sam runs across the road to join the other kids on the beach while she bustles around, filling the morning with her apologies. She's a small bundle of pent-up energy with out-sized glasses and hair that stands out from her head like a clump of tussock. We take the newspapers from the back of the van and plonk them in the porch by the ranch sliders while she unlocks the shed and primes the generator. It roars into life. Once she's unlocked the shop, we all kick off our gumboots and carry the newspapers inside.

I wander between the shelves looking at the same tired old cans.

Stern Discipline instructs me to use my last five dollars to buy meat for the children but Blithe Spirit's thinking chocolate. There's nothing to buy. In the freezer the only packs of meat left cost more than five dollars and the frozen lumps look very unappetising. Blithe Spirit suggests I book it until benefit day but Stern Discipline doesn't hold with that at all.

At the front of the shop Lizzie's getting herself established behind the counter. They're talking about the storm and she's moaning on about some leak Paul hasn't fixed. Eventually I drift back and loiter behind the others.

Flash Kate asks for a packet of Virginia Gold with papers but there's only Port Royal and Pocket Edition left. She decides on Port Royal, which she reckons is so horrible that at least it'll help her cut down. She also takes a newspaper from the pile on the counter.

Big Lou just wants the paper. She glances over the headlines while she waits her turn. "Only two weeks until the election," she marvels. "So soon."

"Guess that's why it's called a snap election," replies Lizzie. She flicks Kate her change and turns to serve Old Tom who's gathered up a flagon of OPG – Old Pale Gold sherry – and the paper and also wants tobacco.

"What do you reckon about having a ball on election night?" she goes on. "You know, everyone'll be out to vote anyway, and it'll be a good chance for us to dress up a bit and lighten this winter gloom."

"Does that mean we'll see you ladies all gussied up for a change?" asks Old Tom, leering lasciviously.

Lizzie and Kate fix him with killing stares while Lou remains absorbed in her newspaper. Old Tom and I often chat when I wander round to the wharf on a low tide. I move back amongst the shelves so I'm not caught up in being mean to him. But he gathers up his stuff and leaves with an irritating chuckle.

Meanwhile Flash Kate's been building up a head of enthusiasm. "What about fancy dress?" she asks. "So we can really express ourselves."

"Dunno ... maybe ..." Despite her glasses Lizzie's sharp blue eyes can pierce right through to your inner space but Kate continues undaunted.

"We used to have fancy dress parties at boarding school. You need a theme though."

High Anxiety starts to churn my stomach until Harshly Critical reminds me that they weren't meaning me. *You won't be invited,* he says, *because Eddie and Angel'll be going for sure.*

"Of course, any input's welcome," Lizzie says. She straightens up the pile of newspapers and realigns the jars of sweets on the shelf by the counter. "Paul will print out invitations for everyone on the post office mailing list when he prints the *Island Eye* next week. It's only two weeks away ... not much time."

"Ooh, can we help? We'd love to, wouldn't we Kate?" Big Lou's hugely excited. "You want to come round later? We'll get some rich ruby for inspiration ... see what we can come up with."

"Why not?" shrugs Lizzie. "Paul's off fishing again and Sam's always rapt to hang out with Marama. I'll come around after I've closed up ... around one. You paying for that port now?"

Big Lou digs seven dollars out of her purse then fossicks out another 69 cents from the pocket of her cardigan.

Flash Kate pours out the contents of her purse on to the counter but only finds five dollars and thirty-one cents. She turns to me. "Are you in, Mouse?" she asks.

I'm feeling the shape of my purse in my Swanni pocket.

Time to leave, shrills High Anxiety.

You should be buying meat for the children, intones Stern Discipline.

Yeah, let's spend the food money on alcohol, sneers Harshly Critical.

But Blithe Spirit's dancing over the sands as I lay my last five dollars on the counter.

Jacob's Bay

The Walshes – Lizzie's father, her mother and her two older sisters – had moved over to Jacob's Bay from the Bay of Plenty back in the fifties when a living could still be made from farming on the island. Lizzie came along the next year. Her birth ended any hope the old man had of a boy to help out as Mrs. Walsh was already forty and had thought her childbearing years were behind her.

The house in Jacob's Bay was substantial. Jacob, a young man full of dreams, had built a one-roomed hut there in the twenties that had grown once a Mrs. Jacob came along and demanded improvements. First there had been an inside bathroom. Bedrooms followed as the family came along, verandahs on three sides of the house and a front room for entertaining with a handsome bay window that looked out over the ocean.

As it goes when one generation succeeds another, Lizzie's father filled in the verandahs over the years. The back was the first to go to make room for a flush toilet and a pantry opening into the kitchen to store the many preserves Mrs. Walsh put by over the summer months. Then the side verandah became a sunroom where she could set up her sewing machine. Finally the front verandah was closed off when Walsh saw the advantages in housing a local telephone exchange.

The handsome bay window survived until the sixties. Farming

had fallen into a bit of a slump by that time so Eddie Elliot opened a small shop over by the wharf to supply bait and groceries to the few holidaymakers who ventured that far out into the gulf. Lizzie's father rose to the challenge. He replaced the bay window with aluminium ranch sliders, sheltered from the prevailing westerlies by a lean-to porch with a window to let in some light, and turned the front room into a general store. Petrol and diesel pumps and a post office that offered banking services turned Jacob's Bay into a centre. This sidelined Eddie Elliot, who moved into firewood although he stayed with bait.

The window was stored in the barn over by the orchard until the early seventies, by which time most of the farm had been cut up and sold off. Walsh had capital in hand and saw an opportunity to boost custom at his shop by way of the summer visitors that Freddie Ladd was regularly flying over to the island in his amphibian. The barn was pulled down and the orchard uprooted. A camping ground with rudimentary washing and cooking facilities was established to provide prospective customers with somewhere to stay. Paddy, over the other side, bought the window for next to nothing.

Lizzie had followed her sisters to boarding school in town over her high school years. At first she came back for holidays but later she moved down to Wellington and there was a long time when the old folk barely heard from her at all. The other girls had also scattered so even her father was not displeased when she returned for Christmas in '78 with a man and a little girl, just turned two.

"Trouble is, the bloke's a queer one," Walsh complained to his wife. "Good for nothing much ... except reading books. They've got some strange ideas too, like those long-haired hippies and their bloody communes."

However his granddaughter Samantha made up for it all. She, at least, adored him. So he enticed them to stay with the offer of a ten-acre block over in the next bay, at a pretty reasonable rate, considering.

The Springbok rugby tour of '81 found Mrs. Walsh caught between the warring factions of the old man – who thought politicians had no business interfering in sport – and the young ones – who were outraged that the Springbok tour was going ahead despite international agreement to oppose apartheid in South Africa. Discontent continued to seethe until Mrs. Walsh finally persuaded her husband to retire to the Bay of Plenty where little Sam could visit in the holidays. Lizzie was already practically running the shop and was happy to lease it off them if she could move back into her old home.

Oh how Lizzie's spirit expanded once she was out of the cramped and very basic Skyline garage on their block and had full control of the shop. Unfortunately, by the end of the first year it was obvious that even the summer trade did not provide enough revenue to stay afloat after the lease had been paid and the costs of building a house on the land were met. If that were ever to be completed, which Paul insisted on, they needed to move back into the garage and rent out her old home.

Around this time Patsy Dervish's normally ebullient spirits were being eroded by the memory of the previous winter's trudge through the mud every morning to get Marama and Ben down to the wharf to catch the school bus on time. It had fallen to her to do the driving most mornings because Big Lou had Gabe still on the tit and Flash Kate had only endured two months of the morning rush before finding somewhere closer to the school to live. As winter closed in she woke up every morning to a sense of impending doom, Patsy confided to Lizzie over the counter one day. Now Patsy and Lizzie had that reciprocal relationship that is common amongst mothers whose children become friends so what could be more obvious than her renting the old homestead?

Everyone agreed it was 'meant to be'. Sam continued to have the run of the house and had someone to hang out with while her mother handled the after-school rush. Lizzie got a tenant who could be trusted to make good use of the shop's recently acquired wine licence and would be available nights to answer any after-hour calls to the telephone exchange. And the Wairua crowd now had a home-away-from-home to visit when they had business at the shop and to stay if they could not make it home after late night partying.

The ladies came out into the porch. Big Lou, a statuesque woman full of vigour, her large frame honed down to bone and muscle, was working a foot into her right gumboot when her flowing patchwork skirt got caught. As she bent down to pull it free, her topknot fell out and her black hair rippled down like water in a rocky creek. With a snort of exasperation she put her newspaper and the port down on the bench beside Flash Kate, who was rolling a cigarette with fervid fingers. She lit it, sustained herself with a lungful of smoke and glanced through the window to see what the children were doing down on the beach.

Thad and Ben, Lou's eldest boy, were fossicking for treasure in the bank of flotsam left by the out-going tide. Ben, a sturdy boy with lank light-brown hair hanging over his eyes, barefooted and wearing a hand-knitted homespun jumper, was trying to extricate a sheet of plywood from the tangle. He called out to Nick to come and help, but Nick, a slighter version of his brother, was looking under rocks for crabs at the far end of the beach where the swollen creek had forced its way through a braided stream, and appeared not to hear.

Lilith, however, was helping with manic enthusiasm, leaping in to grab the very bits Thad was trying to salvage. He stopped to throw her a stick and she bounded down the rain-pocked sand after it, snapped it up and came trotting back to drop it at his feet and stand with her ears pricked and her tail wagging.

He skimmed it down to the firm sand where Marama and Sam were sculpting a fine creation with turrets, tunnels and a moat that would fill up as the tide came in. Lilith careered after the stick, throwing up a fan of sand over the girls as she scooped it up. Sam sprang to her feet, maybe just a moment too soon as if she'd been waiting for the opportunity. She stood, hands firmly planted on plump hips, hair sticking out every which way.

"Ew, Thad!" she yelled. "Your dog's spraying sand all over us!"

Thad and Ben smirked at each other and returned to the job at hand. Lilith trotted sedately back up the beach with her stick. Sam whispered something to Marama who laughed, glancing at the boys from beneath a mop of ginger hair. Her long pale fingers continued plastering the sides of the castle with wet sand from the moat, smoothing it out and patting it to bring the excess water to the surface.

Across the middle of the beach a shallow pool reflected the clearing sky in a slash of silver. Here Melissa and Gabe were making big splashes. They jumped and jumped, shrieking excitedly.

"Oh geez, just look at those two getting all wet again," exclaimed Kate. "There's no way I need any more wet clothes to deal with." She slipped on her boots and ran across the road to the beach.

"Bring them up and we'll put them in the bath before lunch," Big Lou called after her. "The fire's been going all morning so there's lots of hot water."

"Melissa, don't go getting all wet, sweetie. You and Gabe come up now. We'll go back to Patsy's place and get you dried off." Kate's voice cast a thread of melody between the steady beat of the generator and the distant grumble of the sea.

Lou settled the port back on her hip, took up the paper and came out on to the road to add a deeper counterpoint. "You others better come up soon too. It's getting on to lunchtime. You too, Sam."

Mouse, who appeared smaller than she actually was because she was swamped in oversized army pants, khaki Swanndri and a black knitted hat pulled down to over-shadow her brow, had been hovering outside, fists clenched in her pockets, advancing a step or two towards the road and then retreating again. She started edging away, mumbling that she should be off.

Big Lou gazed at her in disgust. "You're such a piker, Mouse. Come on, you've already put in for this." And when Mouse still hesitated she added, "Horse Fly stayed last night. He's probably rolling up as we speak."

The warm kitchen was redolent of freshly baked bread and wood-smoke. Two loaves were cooling on a rack on the clear bench. The floor had been swept and the cushions on the settee were plumped up and tidily arranged. A large ginger cat, seriously engaged in sleeping, lay in one of the armchairs that flanked the wood-stove, purring in harmony with the mutterings of the kettle, the occasional grumbles of the hot water cylinder and the odd burble from a container of fermenting liquor positioned to take advantage of the stove's warmth. The centre of the room was dominated by a large table where Horse Fly sat surrounded by the debris of his breakfast.

Horse Fly had been a jockey until he came down at the bottom of a pile-up and was put out of the running for good. He was a Waikato boy, born and bred, and had planned to set up there when his racing days were behind him: run a smallholding and breed a racehorse or two. However the payout he received from ACC, along with what savings he had, was not enough to see the distance so he consulted a lawyer who just happened to be Pete's brother, John.

John was finalizing the setting up of a land company to buy Wairua. An old church on the Coromandel, which Pete and John attended every Sunday when holidaying with their grandmother, had just come up for tender and removal. Everyone involved with Wairua agreed it would be perfect as a community house but – problem – all the money they had managed to scrape together had gone on buying the land. So they welcomed Horse Fly as a shareholder, secured the tender and, in September '76, they set up camp near the church grounds and began the work of demolition.

It was Christmas before they'd finished demolishing the church, de-nailing the lumber and shipping it across the Hauraki Gulf to the Island in Pete's catamaran. Through the hot summer days and into the autumn they hauled the fragmented church up a dirt track to the land and refashioned it into a community house. Horse Fly's first horse was a Clydesdale; at the other end of the spectrum to the racehorses he had dreamt of breeding, but useful for what needed to be done. At the end of it all, however, Horse Fly decided that communal living was not for him so he spent the winter constructing a hut out of kanuka, punga and corrugated iron over on the next ridge.

Horse Fly had cleared a space amongst the breakfast things – a porridge-encrusted saucepan, a large peanut butter jar serving as a milk jug, a teapot in a stained cosy, a big Milo tin painted blue and labelled *sugar*, a bowl, a spoon and a mug. An open Dubbin tin – half-filled with marijuana – a depleted packet of Virginia Gold, a yellow packet of cigarette papers, a silver lighter and a scallop shell with a couple of butts in it formed an inner circle. His large and bulbous nose, misshapen from a lifetime of brawling, lurked in the shadow of a shapeless felt hat as he crumbled a head onto the stack of cyclostyled paper that was last month's *Island Eye*. It darted nervously towards the door when he heard it opening but it was only Lou with some other ladies and a surge of cold air.

Big Lou snatched up the porridge pot, threw it with a clang into the sink and filled it with water. Then she fell into a steady, domestic rhythm – opening the draughts on the stove, stoking the fire, adding more wood, filling the kettle, shifting the plate from above the fire to expose the kettle to the naked flame, pulling a large soup pot forward on to the second plate.

Disturbed by the clatter, the cat opened one eye, moved an ear back, flicked his tail and slipped into sleep again, although a glint of eye still showed and his ear remained back. Only when Kate chivvied the children closer to the fire, stripped off their wet clothes and settled them on the wood-box wrapped in a crocheted blanket did it become altogether too much for the cat. It jumped off the armchair and stalked over to the backdoor.

Horse Fly finished breaking up the head and stuck two cigarette papers together. He glared at the door in the corner between the hot-water cupboard and the bench that Kate had left open when she went through to start running a bath for the children. Lou moved to close it but Kate was already returning with a pile of books to keep the children amused.

Mouse lingered by the backdoor, oblivious to the cat's round orange eyes staring up at her. She was taking in the Maori land-march poster above the settee, the moon calendar hanging on the back of the door that Kate had just come through, the hearth-rug knotted up out of discarded t-shirts and the crystals arranged on the windowsill, twinkling in the light from the window above the kitchen sink.

"You going to sit down?" asked Lou. She moved past her to let the cat out.

Mouse slid into the chair closest to the door. She pretended to be watching her thumbs move around one another in her lap but really she was following Horse Fly's progress. He sealed the joint and laid it beside Lou's newspaper lying in the centre of the table.

Kate sat down opposite him. She pulled the paper closer to peruse the headlines.

"Muldoon's borrowing another 660 million dollars from the Japanese," she noted. "Wouldn't you think he'd wait, now he's called this election?"

"More think-big projects to destroy the environment with," muttered Mouse.

"Obviously he thinks National's going to win again. They won't though, will they?" Lou asked from the sink where she was mixing up more milk. She gazed out the window at the washing swaying languidly on a line stretched out between the woodshed and a macrocarpa tree that lounged beside the patch of emerald grass above the septic tank. Lizzie's cow grazed over in the camping ground.

Kate's fingers beat out a quick rhythm on the paper. "Doubt it. It's not like he's got all those rabid rugby fans roused up this time. Surely all those rednecks won't be enough to get him in for a fourth term."

"My old man loves him. He's got rich on all the farm subsidies Piggy hands out," said Lou. She put the milk jar beside the four mugs lined up on the table and moved to the stove to make the tea.

"And he's not the only one. Lots of people out there do," she added.

"Yeah, all those rich fuckers who're creaming it," put in Horse Fly.

"And just as many can't stand him." Kate pushed the paper away and got up to check on the bath water. "I'll be very surprised if Labour doesn't win. Lange's very popular. Ooh, I can't wait … and a ball, too." She opened the door and pirouetted through it, "What fun!"

"Ball?" repeated Horse Fly. He glanced at Lou to see how close she was to joining them.

"Lizzie's putting on a ball," Lou explained. "Two weeks away – on election night."

"A fancy dress," Kate called through the open door above the sound of cold water gushing into the bath.

"I'm not going if I have to dress up." Horse Fly extracted the racing pages from the paper, shook them open and retired behind them.

"Ah, don't be such a stuffy old coot. We could do with a bit of fun," scoffed Lou. She stood back to check that all was in order: the teapot in its cosy, the jar of milk, the sugar tin and the line of mugs.

"Lizzie's coming over later and we're going to make plans," she said taking the empty kettle to the sink to refill it. "See we've even bought some port for inspiration." She gestured at the flagon standing on the bench beside the loaves of bread and then paused to consult the moon calendar on her way back to the stove.

"I wonder what the moon'll be doing. Wow… heady times. It's the day after the Capricorn full moon when Saturn goes direct. And on the actual day … get this … Venus moving into Leo … it says, 'drama, flamboyance in affections'. Shit hot! It'll really go off! Let's hope it's fine."

"Not likely," came a gloomy pronouncement from behind the racing pages.

Lou plumped down in the chair nearest the stove with a sigh.

Horse Fly clamped his lizard lips around the joint and flicked his lighter. The flame angled towards the joint as he sucked on it. "When's Patsy coming back?" he asked through smoke-filled lungs.

"Tomorrow's Sea Bee, I reckon," Lou replied. "She's staying with her sister in Ponsonby."

This brought a loud splutter of laughter from Flash Kate who was coming back into the room. "Oh ye-a-h," she drawled. "Like she was 'gunna' come back last week and like Pete was 'gunna' be back last Wednesday."

"Here you kids, your bath's ready."

"Reckon she'll come back with Pete... Tuesday, Wednesday at the latest, now the weather's cleared," mused Horse Fly once Kate had herded the children into the bathroom. "That mad bitch wouldn't fly if she could get home for free."

Lou drew on the joint and leant forward to hand it across to Mouse, who was waiting for it with barely concealed impatience. She poured milk into the mugs, twirled the teapot three times to the right and twice to the left and began to pour the tea.

"Well, Belle'll probably lend her the money... same thing really," Lou finally replied. "I'm pretty certain she'll be home tomorrow though. You know, don't you, when someone's coming home? You can sort of feel their thoughts or something."

"Yeah," put in Mouse on an expelled breath. "We get that in Fissure too, if someone's been away and they're coming back. You're not really thinking about them at all and then one day they're just there, in your head, all day. Like they're kind of reaching forward in their thoughts to finger out a place to settle in."

The joint circulated in silence until Kate returned and the conversation turned to cows, hens and gardens.

Horse Fly reported that things were pretty lean up home. The hens were still off the lay and there was not much more than silver beet in the garden. "Plenty of pigs about though," he added.

Lou said that Patsy's hens were starting to redden up, so they would soon be laying, and there were plenty of vegetables. "I was hoping Lizzie's cow would calve before Patsy got back. She's going to share the milking. I miss milking." She launched into an enthusiastic rave about the joys of milking, her fingers curling as she spoke as if around a cow's teats.

Horse Fly told them once again about going to milk on cold Waikato mornings, how he would stand in the fresh cowpats to warm his feet.

The ladies sipped their tea and made no reply.

"Dutchie's cow's been milking for over a week now," Lou continued after a pause. "I was just taking a banana cake out of the oven, Lizzie had a special on over-ripe bananas when he dropped in with some cream. It was a few days ago... before the storm. He hung around until the kids came home from school to help us eat it."

"Oh yeah?" Kate was carefully noncommittal.

But then the back door banged open and a flurry of movement filled the room. Hungry voices were demanding to be fed.

As soon as they had been fed and watered the older children rushed down the passage past the bathroom and out through the sunroom into the garden. Earlier, Thad and Ben had roped Nick in to give them a hand to carry their collection of lumber up from the beach and now they planned to launch it all into the creek that ran along the bottom of the garden. Marama and Sam scurried off in the direction of the camping ground to check out a secret place Marama had found. They had been whispering about building a hut there all through lunch.

The women sloughed off their outer garments and arranged themselves on the sunroom steps taking in the sun. Horse Fly sprawled behind them close enough to eavesdrop while he read the newspaper. The little ones were settled on the bed in the sunroom where they soon dropped off to sleep.

Lizzie, had arrived just as they finished lunch and was now perched on the second step, looking over the garden. "Look how overgrown it's getting," she said wistfully. "That's what happens when you take on tenants, I suppose. Still, at least Patsy's kept the vege garden going."

"I like it wild like this," said Big Lou. The port and five disparate glasses were lined up beside her in the doorway. "I did weed around the spring bulbs just after Patsy left but it's been so wet."

A high hedge on the seaward side sheltered the garden from the prevailing westerly and the road. It was one of those old gardens that could have been growing forever, a riot of shrubs and perennials striving for their place in the sun. Everywhere the spring bulbs were spearing upward and there was already a whiff of jonquil in the air. In the centre winter vegetables stood in ordered rows: silverbeet, broccoli, leeks, turnips, carrots and broad beans that were not yet in flower. Various herbs sprawled around the perimeter. On the landward side of the house a large grapefruit tree dropped yellow fruit beside the henhouse. The hens were out, scratching and pecking amongst the shrubbery, feeding on worms driven to the surface by the rising water table.

Lou poured the port and handed it around while Lizzie filled them in on gossip from the shop. A boat had broken its mooring during the storm. Another chap was trying to get to town for the birth of his child.

"Oh and there was a slip on the hill road," she went on after they had mulled over these events. "That's why I was late with the papers this morning." She glanced at Horse Fly. "Some late-stayers at the Surf Club were trapped there overnight."

"How desperate would you be to go over there last night?" Kate pondered aloud. "The weather was so foul."

"Only real staunch buggers," broke in Horse Fly. "Me and Dutchie were over that side anyway. Lucky we left early before the slip."

"Because of the fight?" asked Lizzie.

"Fight?" echoed Big Lou.

The women all looked at Horse Fly with interest.

"With the McLaren boys? Yeah... didn't come to much." He returned to the paper whistling tunelessly to himself.

In the warm afternoon bees hummed busily at their patches. Out on the shore a wave broke and the sound receded along the beach.

"This Bob Jones is a good bloke," Horse Fly said at last. "Been in the boxing scene for years. Reckon he'll get my vote."

Big Lou bristled. "The 'treat-women-like-dogs' man? Firmness and flattery? Fucking chauvinist."

"What's this?" asked Lizzie.

"Bob Jones said in an interview the other day that the way to treat women was how you treat dogs," Kate told her, "with a mixture of firmness and flattery."

"Bastard!" Lizzie crouched over her knees, clasping her socked toes.

"Ah, who needs men anyway?" said Kate. "You could waste your whole life hanging around waiting for them. Still you're lucky with Paul," she gushed. "He's so devoted to Sam and look at that lovely house he's building. It's so artistic."

"Yeah, well... if it's ever finished." Lizzie thrust her fingers into her hair and worked out some knots. "Since Rueben's been in town it takes Paul all day to row over and feed his bloody hens... which aren't even laying, I might add." She tussled with a particularly tight tangle.

"There's no way I wanted to spend another winter in the garage," she continued once it was free, "and yet here we are. We can't even hear the radio above the sound of the rain on the roof and there's this leak... at least he could fix that." She drained her glass and put it down beside the flagon. "Ah well ... what can you do? Let's talk about the ball."

Big Lou topped up everyone's glass while Lizzie recounted that there was a lull in custom because of the weather on Thursday so Rose and her had played Scrabble.

"Richie was there too," she added. "He insisted on playing, although he's hopeless really."

"What, Richie Rich?" asked Flash Kate, "The American Dream?"

"The same," smirked Lizzie. "He's been hanging around here a lot lately ... guess he must've done all the ladies over on the other side."

"Go on, he's got the hots for Patsy, is what it is," laughed Lou.

Vengeful mutterings about the Yank being a nark and what Willie's cousin's mate, who was over here last summer, reckoned were heard behind them.

"You know what it is," Lizzie explained. "Nothing to break the monotony of winter. I was doing a moan to Richie about the boringness of it all when it came to me … a mid-winter ball! It'll do us all a power of good to have a big occasion, a chance to dress up, something a bit over the top. And everyone'll be coming out of the woodwork to vote so it makes sense to have it that weekend."

"But won't people want see who wins?" objected Kate.

"So we'll have a radio going in the supper room or something," Lizzie snapped. "That's hardly a big issue. And the fishing club has the hall on Saturday nights so we'll be able to use their liquor license – save getting a special one. Rose'll propose it at their meeting on Monday night."

"It should be a fancy dress," insisted Kate, "so we can give full rein to our fantasies. We need a theme though."

Horse Fly took out his tin and rolled another number. It passed from hand to hand as they thought about the possibilities.

"What about a vice versa?" suggested Kate. "You know, where you dress up as the opposite sex."

Horse Fly choked on the joint. "You won't have any blokes there then. You ladies might want to be blokes but none of us want to be women."

"I thought you weren't going anyway," retorted Big Lou.

"That's no good," said Lizzie. "I want to get all dolled up. Maybe we could have an historic theme. I rather fancy myself as Marie Antoinette."

"Where'd we get the dresses from though?" Lou demurred.

"You must all have dresses, surely," exclaimed Lizzie. "I want to express my hidden side – let the she-wolf out for an airing."

"Wouldn't have thought she-wolves wore dresses," grunted Horse Fly.

The faint cries of the boys down by the creek drifted up to them against the busy murmur of water on the move. The shadows were lengthening as the sun skimmed the ridge-line.

Suddenly Mouse said, "I thought of a song last night."

Lizzie, who had forgotten Mouse was sitting on the bottom step, jumped slightly.

"A song?" Flash Kate repeated turning around to stare at Mouse.

"Um ...er ...yeah." Mouse had her hands clenched in her trouser pockets and huddled back against the baluster behind her.

"Well, let's hear it then," said Big Lou craning to see around Lizzie.

"What ... you mean now?"

"Only if you want to," said Lizzie kindly.

After an initial hesitation, a grimace and a swallow Mouse, her eyes fixed on a dandelion poking out from beneath the step, began to sing in a wavering voice that strengthened as she got through the first lines:

Well, we skip though the trees
With the greatest of ease,
First on our bottoms,
And then on our knees.
The dishes aren't done
And the beds are unmade,
And all life is,
Is a pattern of shades.

"Huh, that's quite good," said Lizzie.

"I didn't know you were musical," remarked Kate.

"There's a kinda gumboot dance, like the Chesdale cheese ad, that goes with it," Mouse explained. "Sort of like this," she says standing up and demonstrating.

"Let's give it a go," cried Big Lou.

The four ladies linked arms and step, step, kicked as they picked up the words of the song. When it was over they fell about with laughter.

"Hey, it's good to see you girls enjoying yourselves," drawled a voice. Richie, all blond curls and perfect dentistry, was emerging from the shrubbery at the bottom of the garden followed by three muddy boys.

The ladies adjusted their clothing and Lou tied up her topknot, which had fallen down while they were dancing. Lizzie smoothed down her recalcitrant mop and gave him a bright smile.

"Where did you spring from, sneaking up on us like that?"

"Just came over to see how you were getting on. I've brought alcohol. What was that song you were singing? It sounded like fun."

But Mouse had retired into herself, huddled on the bottom step, and now the little ones were waking up. Melissa sat on her mother's lap, whining and clinging, while Lilith competed for Kate's attention by thrusting her nose between them. Marama and Sam emerged from the campground, giggling mysteriously between themselves and casting sidelong looks at the boys, who were staging a grapefruit fight. The rooster led his bevy of hens in a chorus of cackling. It was time to start feeding and watering all over again.

The Well

The back door clicks, jerking me out of my cavern of sleep. Harshly Critical's laugh tramps through my brain like footsteps over gravel.

Horse Fly!

The name slides down my throat and settles in my stomach like a lump of cold porridge; a thought so dire that I am driven down into the darkness again.

When Stern Discipline finally urges me awake the sun's rays have already penetrated the boatshed and High Anxiety's all of a witter about the pile of housework that needs doing before the girls come home. When I sit up my brain sloshes around in my skull making me nauseous and a stink of spent sex surges up from my sticky maw. I lie back again and sink into the *shush-drag* rhythm of ripples caressing the shingle at the tide's edge.

Stern Discipline is stiff-backed and full of censure. *Grain and Vine Don't Combine,* he rants, glaring down at me from his high perch.

Then High Anxiety remembers the song and I'm hiding under the covers from the shame of it all.

Sensing weakness Harshly Critical goes in for the kill. *Stupid! They'll be getting some laughs out of you today, that's for sure.*

I turn over and look down from my loft at the dark tunnel that is my life. Dust motes dance in the oblique rectangles of sunlight falling through the two sets of louvre windows spaced along the north-facing wall.

Housework, decrees Stern Discipline.

At least I made a start after Eddie left on Friday. The girls' mess has been tidied away into the fish-bins under their bunks, the dishes are stacked up beside the sink and the remainder of the washing has been sorted into piles. I maneuver my fragile form down the ladder and seat it once again on my beer-crate in the sun. I feed water, drop by drop, into my cesspit stomach.

The first time I slept with that slimy turd, Horse Fly, was during the long winter the girls and I spent alone in Fissure Bay. We were both lonely souls and I thought sharing our bodies might ease the cravings. It didn't. The second time was at Wairua when I was sleeping-over after a party. He found me lost in a dream amongst the lumped bodies and I didn't realize he came from the real world until it was too late.

Last night we played five hundred until Richie's bourbon ran out. Big Lou and Richie were partners against Flash Kate and me. Horse Fly sat by the fire and strummed Patsy's guitar, stopping from time to time to roll another joint. He reckoned he never played cards unless it was for money.

I'm trying to remember what happened next. Horse Fly must have got a ride with Kate because I remember being cramped up in the back with the kids and Lilith's wet nose poking me from the floor as she tried to angle herself a place on the seat. Then he insisted on helping me down the track, just because I'd fallen over – well yes, okay, a couple of times.

Several times, breaks in Harshly Critical. *You were legless!*

I can remember how he banged on for hours. I tried faking orgasms but it didn't change a thing so I got what sleep I could while he finished whatever steeplechase it was he was riding.

Slut! shrieks Harshly Critical into my pounding head. *That's the only sex someone like you deserves!*

Stern Discipline's mourning the five dollars I put in for the port. *The girls would have liked some meat for dinner tonight. Now what's it going to be? Rice again, I suppose!*

But all this is obliterated when High Anxiety remembers the song and the floorshow Lizzie decided we should do for the ball: yesterday before she headed home. We're to get together Tuesday to talk about it. My head slumps to my knees, is cradled in my arms.

You needn't worry, jeers Harshly Critical. *Flash Kate's taken charge. She'll have a much better idea that won't include you. She'll have had dancing lessons as a child, you can be sure.*

With Stern Discipline keeping a firm hold on my stomach I work my way through the water and soon feel well enough to light the outside fire. It's so sodden that, even after I've scraped out the old ashes and set it with dry brush and twigs from under the tank stand, I have to reset it three times before it will maintain a sullen flame. While I wait for the fire to take hold and heat up some water for the dishes I boil the kettle on the gas ring inside and roll a joint to enjoy with a cup of tea.

The joint brings out Blithe Spirit, leaping and prancing on centre stage. *This is how it'll be when you sing your song to the world,* she cries. *The spotlight will warm your skin. The scent of bouquets will fill your nostrils. Applause will thunder around you. Everyone will love you ... especially Paul. And even ...* here her voice lowers to a stage whisper ... *maybe even Richie.*

Oh Richie, with his hooded eyes and his oh-so-kissable lips that twitch when he's suppressing laughter at our odd island ways. My body cries out to be pillowed against his surf-hardened chest.

Harshly Critical falls about laughing at the notion. *You?* he gasps. *You, who Horse Fly uses as a blow-up doll?*

The water's boiling now. Stern Discipline draws me back to the job in hand. *The fire needs stoking and you'd better put some rice on ... and bake some bread, seeing as you didn't buy any meat to make a nice stew. You need a bath too.*

I pour the water into the kitchen sink, refill the pot, put it back on the plate with the kettle on the one side and a pot of rice on the other. I feed the fire with some more driftwood and then return to the kitchen to start on the dishes. While I swish the cutlery around in the water Blithe Spirit, excited by the prospect of finally making some friends, conjures up scenarios of confidences over morning tea, late night raves, shared dinners and communal childcare.

They like you, she whispers, *and they like your song. You'll be one of them if you go through with this. You won't be weirdo Mouse any more. You'll be the woman who made up that song.*

Tuh, they're laughing at you, counters Harshly Critical. *All those silences and exchanged looks. You're just too simple to realize what's going on.*

The Wairua women are scary in their casual capability. They have no time for anyone who can't keep up. Eddie told me all about them before we moved over. He'd often stayed at Wairua when he was spending time the previous summer at Fissure Bay and was sure I would be as impressed by them as he was. Men, of course, know nothing about dynamics between women.

Patsy Dervish is said to have come up with the name *Wairua*. They wanted something Maori to reflect the indigenous quality of their ideals and Patsy Dervish knows all about things Maori. She's always talking about when she was sixteen, ran away from home and lived in a shed belonging to an old Maori woman down on the Coromandel. She thinks using words like *mimi* and *kai* gives her some kind of credibility the rest of us don't have. I don't know much about Maoris at all, although I remember we once did poi dancing at Primary School.

Wairua means 'spirit'. Patsy chose it because of the unseen force that animates the air around Wairua. It's really just the bush. We feel it much stronger in Fissure Bay where the bush is way thicker. But then I guess that that old church they have for a community house adds to the spiritual dimension of the place … gives them that sense of closeness.

Not like all you people from Fissure, sneers Harshly Critical, *who can't stand to even be in the same room together.*

We're a mixed bunch at Fissure Bay, some of us more interested in growing marijuana than in creating a lifestyle for the future. Kate and Patsy seem to be able to hold things together, whereas the split between Angel and I is irreversible. Of course Patsy flits like a bumblebee from male to male and was well finished with Pete when Kate came on the scene. It was different with Eddie and me.

At the end of our first summer at Fissure Bay I took the girls back to

Orewa to spend the winter with my family. I didn't find it that pleasant. My mother and I have issues. I never can quite measure up to darling Louisa, two years older than me and doing so well in London. Tracey started school and I made myself helpful in my father's chemist shop but I missed the bush terribly. I couldn't wait for September when we could move back.

Eddie was glad to see us and life seemed to carry on as normal. It was Christmas time before I realized that when he and Angel went off into the bush together they were doing something other than getting firewood. Over dinner, down on the beach – a feed of crayfish, paua, assorted salads and some new potatoes, Angel announced she was pregnant. It took all my concentration on breaking open a crayfish leg and drawing out the flesh inside to bury my pain and humiliation.

Once it was out in the open she couldn't keep her hands off him, always cuddling up to him while I was around, rubbing in the fact that she was in possession now. I tried so hard to handle it. After all an anarchist can't complain that other people are breaking the rules. I know all that about how nobody owns anyone. And she was nice to the girls when the baby was growing inside her. She even took care of them sometimes so I could go out into the world by myself.

They went to stay with his parents in May while they waited for the birth. Eddie's family's in construction and they own a large house on the beachfront at Orewa. We could've gone back too but the solitude had already started to engulf me and I knew I was not strong enough to face up to it all. Our parents are old friends. I pictured my mother's face – the down-turned lips, the lowered eyes that would face me across the breakfast table every morning.

Throughout the long winter we lived alone in the community house. The encroaching and subsiding of the waves marked the tempo of our daily routine. When the sky cleared, we went fishing or for walks in the bush. When it rained, we sat around the wood stove working on Tracey's correspondence and the pre-school stuff they sent Janey. Sometimes we drew and we played a lot of cards and read. Occasionally Trev, who had his own place further up the gully, would drop in some fish or pork but other than him we barely saw another soul, except for once a month when we trekked out to the shop and spent a night at Wairua with Big Lou and her boys. I was content enough, I guess, but lonely. It was during a long winter night, lying awake listening to the loud shrieks and moans of the spirits partying in the bush, that I named the dragons that filled my mind. At first I was glad of the conversation but they've come to dominate my life and I don't know how to get rid of them.

One day Eddie stepped out of the bush. I ran to give him a welcoming hug but he pushed me away. Everything had changed. From then on the girls could do nothing right, all my fault, of course. I was bringing them up all wrong. Angel wasn't going to allow little Jesse to spread his toys through the hut like that, refuse to eat his porridge or speak to her the way Tracey spoke to me. No doubt she'll find out the truth in time. Boys are hard going, to judge from the ones I see around me.

It was around harvest time that I finally broke. Marijuana was plentiful and maybe I was getting stoned more than was good for me. Whatever the cause, one morning over breakfast Angel and I had a big blow-up. I can't even remember what it was about now, only that I threw the contents of the porridge pot at her, well not at her, you understand, but in her direction. Porridge splattered over all over the place, up the walls, across the floor. Eddie was very angry with me. They all turned against me then ... so I had to leave ... and now I'm an exile.

Here, you're getting a bit weepy, says Stern Discipline. *Your blood sugar must be getting low. Best put on a couple of potatoes to cook while the bread's rising.*

I leave the rest of the dishes soaking in the sink and mix up some molasses, yeast and warm water, leaving it to prove while I go outside to scrub some potatoes in the outside tub that's not filled with washing.

The day's not getting any younger, Stern Discipline warns. *That washing has to be done.*

Once the rice has been moved off the plate to the back of the fire pit and the potatoes put in its place, I don rubber gloves and sink my hands into the slimy mess which is the soaking washing. That has no sooner been fed through the wringer than I remember the yeast, so I leave the washing soaking in the rinsing water and go back inside again to mix up the bread. But then, there are the dishes, still not finished. I work on steadily until the bread is set aside in the camp-oven to rise, the dishes are neatly stacked in the beer-crate and plank shelves, the washing drips on the line and I've followed the sun over to the bank by the fire-pit with my bowl of potatoes.

The fire has developed a good bed of embers that sends up a thin stream of smoke. On the empty beach a couple of oystercatchers are pottering around, probing under rocks with their long orange beaks. A car, heading towards the wharf, stitches a thread of sound through the silence. Taties are such comfort food when their warm fluffiness is mixed with lashings of butter, some garlic and parsley for flavour and a good sprinkling of savoury yeast to boost the vitamin B in an excess-ravaged stomach.

While I eat I think about where I could start a garden. I so miss having a garden to potter around in and all those fresh vegetables. The silver beet and parsley I planted against the boat-shed wall when we first moved in are growing well and there's a succulent patch of puha around the tank-stand on the other side of the shed but there's no room for anything else. The only flat area is above the fire-pit and that's right by the long-drop. The washing line stretches across it over to a scraggly green-weed that has populated the rest of the slope with its progeny.

Why bother with a garden at all? sulks Harshly Critical. *You're going to have to move out for the summer in any case.*

Out of the blue distance a small black speck grows into the Sea Bee. It follows a descending path beyond the point down into Jacob's Bay.

Must be two o'clock, comments Stern Discipline. *If you hurry with your bath you'll have time to consult the I Ching about the song before the kids come home.*

I relight the joint I had started earlier and begin to feel better.

Maybe Eddie'll stop for a chat when he drops the kids off like he did on Friday, suggests Blithe Spirit,

Nah, he'd just come out of the bush and was starved for company, replies Harshly Critical. *He'll be wanting to get on now he's been cuddling up to Angel all weekend.*

We had such a good time on that Friday, remembering when we were teenagers hanging out together at the Golf Club while our parents competed for dinner sets and boxes of crystal glassware. We were boyfriend and girlfriend in my final year at school. He'd already joined his two older brothers in the construction company that was growing with the town. I felt so grown up having a boyfriend who had money to spend.

The next year I started at University and lived in the hostel because the commute from Orewa was too long. What heady times they were; living away from home for the first time, free from the confines of my family. I began to discover who I really was. I would have left Eddie behind if Tracey hadn't taken root inside me when we drifted together again over summer. He wanted me more than I wanted him then. Now I'm grateful for a shared joint and a simple conversation.

But now you've got the song, Blithe Spirit soothes. *Everyone will love you now you've got the song.* All happy-eyed and bouncy, she swirls around her feather boa and showers down rose petals from her airy pedestal. Things are starting to look shipshape again. There's enough rice cooked for the next two days and the bread can go on as soon as my bath water's heated.

You should have got that washing out first thing this morning, growls Stern Discipline. *It'll never dry now and what if it rains tomorrow?*

The washing drips limply on the line.

Tomorrow will be fine, Blithe Spirit reassures me. *Things go in threes. The third wave's always the biggest and you can always count on three fine days in a row.*

But now High Anxiety's all worried that Angel hasn't put the girls in the bath and what if it isn't fine tomorrow? They won't get to bath until the next break in the weather. *Oh it's all so easy for her with a wood-stove, gravity-fed water and an actual bath.*

Harshly Critical goes off on to a rant about what a dreadful mother I am, expecting other people to keep my children clean. He goes on to contemplate what dreadful thing I must have done in a past lifetime to end up here, living in a boat-shed with no hot water and two children who can't stay out of the mud.

Here, that water's getting hot. Stern Discipline breaks in. *You'll feel much better once you've washed.*

I wash my hair first and then crouch in the tub with my knees under my chin. Ah it feels so good to sink my nether regions into the warm water. The camp oven sits in the scattered fire covered in embers. The dishes and one load of washing are done. There'll be rice and bread for the days ahead and, if it's fine tomorrow, I can get another load of washing out when this lot finally dries. Considering the start to the day I haven't done too badly. Maybe there's even time left for an *I Ching* reading.

I selected the 50 manuka sticks I use for the *I Ching* out of the brush pile back in Fissure Bay and stripped the bark off them. Constant use has built up a patina making them smooth against my palm. I sit cross-legged facing the sea. The sun, hovering above the northwestern horizon, shines through the windows in the loft. Already the shadows are starting to lengthen. The question in my mind struggles to find a form.

When Blithe Spirit has the floor, I'm excited about the song. This could be the next step out of the abyss of isolation and despair I am drowning in. However it doesn't take long for High Anxiety to drag me back down into the mire she inhabits. There I flounder, hiding from the searing lash of Harshly Critical's scorn.

"How can this song help me?" I intone and count out 49 sticks, laying the last aside on the paper that I've found to draw the hexagram on. I divide the stack into two, put one stick from the right-hand pile between the ring and little finger on my left hand and begin counting the left-hand pile out in fours.

Despite all Stern Discipline's efforts to get me to focus, my mind flows all over the place when I'm counting out the sticks. It's not long before I'm wondering what possessed me to sing my song to the ladies like that.

Because you're a drunken slut, Harshly Critical breaks in with a bray of derision.

The scene plays over and over in my mind until High Anxiety shrouds me in murk.

I place the remaining three sticks between my ring and middle finger and start counting out the right-hand pile.

Blithe Spirit reminds me that even Richie liked the song, the little bit he heard of it.

Yeah, except you were too cowardly to sing it again, Harshly Critical loses no time in reminding me. *There's no way you'll ever sing it in public.*

High Anxiety tugs me down again, down to the safety of her swamp.

The remaining sticks join those between my fingers to make the first pile. I lay them aside and gather up the rest to divide again. A pile of eight and then another pile of eight, all the time tussling with the dragons over the song while I count out in fours. The three piles represent a broken line, which I draw on my paper, clear the dragons from my mind and start again.

Lizzie floats into view. She's such a dominating woman. Maybe she really could take on Flash Kate and win. I certainly wouldn't want to cross her. And yet ... and I wander off into a dream of Paul.

A pile of nine sticks and two of four represent an unbroken line to draw above the broken one. Then five and two fours form a line that moves from an unbroken to a broken one, which I note by drawing a circle through the line. This line gives me an extra verse to ponder and goes to form a further hexagram as well.

Even though I clear my mind, every time I stop to draw a line it soon takes off in another direction: the song, Lizzie, Paul, Flash Kate, Wairua, Fissure Bay, Eddie and Angel, the song, Paul.

The Tao of Physics absorbs me while I count out the sixth and final line. I've been reading it most of the last week when I wasn't hiding under the covers. Even though I kept going back and rereading whole passages I still don't really understand what the big deal is about waves and particles or how they can even know all this if they can't see what they are theorizing about.

Loser! screeches Harshly Critical. *You don't understand it at all. You wouldn't even be reading it if you didn't fancy Paul.*

And yet ... I really enjoy the strange places it takes me to.

The first hexagram is *The Well*, which, the moving line tells me, has been cleaned but nobody drinks from it.

This is my heart's sorrow,
For one might draw from it.
If the king were clear-minded,
Good fortune may be joined in common.

There are dangers attached to *The Well*: that the rope may not go down far enough to draw up the clear water or that the jug may break.

This hexagram moves into *The Abysmal*; water doubled. It is a deep ravine where water flows, filling up each depression before it flows on to reach its goal: depression after depression after depression. But what if the water gets trapped in a stagnant pool, as happens sometimes in the creek at Fissure Bay, when only a storm will flush it clean? Tears well up. I close my eyes, draw a deep breath and lie back against my pillows.

A blank wall stares back at me. I've been drawing pictures with coloured pencils to hang there but every new moon, the last one was Friday, I take them down to clear a space for more. Maybe I should start drawing pictures of my readings, start off in a new direction.

A piercing shriek and a pounding of feet brings my alone-time to an end. Jancy bursts through the door, clutching her battered one-eared bear to her chest with one arm while she slams the door shut with the other.

"Mummy! Mummy!" she cries from the middle of the room. "Mummy, where are you? You've got to save Boo Boo. Tracey's going to throw him into the sea and drown him!"

Tracey strolls through the door scowling. "She should throw it away," she snarls. "She's such an embarrassment. The kids at school are all laughing at her. Boo Boo! Boo Hoo more like!"

"Shut the door, Tracey. You're letting the cold in." I climb down from the loft, sit on the bottom bunk and draw Janey to me. "Please don't start fighting as soon as you get home. Don't cry, Love. Tracey's just teasing you. She knows how precious Boo Boo is to you."

Janey burrows her head into my shoulder. Her little body moulds into mine. I smooth down her russet curls.

"How about I make you a nice hot cup of Milo and you can tell me all about your weekend with Daddy?"

Tracey continues to stand at the table glaring at me.

"Is Daddy coming down?" I ask her.

"He just dropped us off 'cause he was running late. He and Angel had a big fight."

"Really? What about?" I ask, quelling Harshly Critical's crowing.

"Us, of course," answers Tracey. "What else do they ever fight about? It's Janey. She's such a crybaby."

"What's for dinner? Rice again, I suppose."

See, sneers Harshly Critical. *Away from you all weekend and all you can offer them when they get back is rice.*

But now they're both smiling.

Tracey pulls a newspaper package from her backpack. "Not!" she cries triumphantly. "Pork chops. Daddy and Trev got a pig."

Returns

The moon moving into Leo in the early hours of Sunday morning swept Lou up in its playful energy. As soon as breakfast was over she jollied the boys along to get the Beast Machine, her Holden station wagon, packed up before the Sea Bee landed so they could get back up the Wairua track before dark.

It was best, she decided, to store most of their stuff in Patsy's spare bedroom: only take the bare necessities in case things all fell apart again. Three weeks of mod cons powered by the shop's generator, which needed to run four hours every day to keep the freezer cold, may well have spoilt her for the bush. The twin-tub, tumble-dry washing machine, the tapes she played while she danced through the housework, the inside toilet, were all luxuries that had allowed her to slip into some very indolent habits. Often she lay in as late as seven in the morning.

And it was so very social. There was always someone dropping in for a cup of tea when they came to the shop. Often, on afternoons when the weather kept customers away, Lizzie would tap on the kitchen wall and she would go around to the shop to spend the afternoon playing Scrabble with Lizzie and Rose.

Rose had even dragged her off to the Women's Division's monthly meeting the previous Tuesday. Ma McLaren, who was a Women's Division stalwart and generally never acknowledged her, chatted away like she was one of them while they waited for the Sea Bee. She was off to Sydney to visit her daughter, the first time in five years she had been off the island. "How lovely it had been to see Lou dressing up for a change and doing her hair so nicely," she went on, eyeing Lou's corduroys and tight-bound plait. Lou shuffled the rocks at her feet and was glad when the Sea Bee finally splashed down and trundled up the beach towards them.

Patsy Dervish slumped down the steps from the Sea Bee, her eyes staring out of sunken pits in her jaundiced skin. Even the mighty frizz of red hair had lost its yeast. Marama rushed into her arms and they clung together while Lou gathered up Patsy's pack and they trooped off back to the house.

All afternoon words spilled out of Patsy's mouth: the nights at the Gluepot, the parties on Waiheke, the flea markets she had been to and the scores she had made, the drugs, the blokes, on and on, over and over, like water from an overflowing tank during a squall. Lou listened and nodded. They would have to stay one more night. All this gabble was covering a deeper pain. Only when the kids had been fed, bathed and bedded, and they were settled in front of the stove with the brandy Patsy had brought back with her, would the truth come out.

The memory of a lost 16-year-old, suffering the sickness of early pregnancy, clinging to Pete's arm as if he was all that was keeping her from floating off into space, has helped Big Lou excuse the many excesses Patsy has indulged in over the years. She remembered the wild bush of red hair, sequined with droplets of water from the drizzly May morning, the shapeless black woollen garment that shrouded the rest of Patsy's body and the pair of scuffed basketball boots that connected her, toe to toe, to the ground. Her head was lowered against her chest and she never looked up once while Pete explained their situation and accepted Lou's offer of a cuppa before she showed them around the house.

After three years in the nurses' residence, Lou had been lucky enough to get a room in a bungalow close to Greenlane hospital, already frequented by a bevy of other nurses. However the riotous times came to an end when one had an Easter wedding and the other two set off on their great OE. The hangers-on drifted away and Lou was left with an empty house.

A good month of mourning and earnest Tarot readings followed before she was able to appreciate the advantages of living alone but by this time her bank account was depleted. Even the pay-rise that came with promotion to sister of the cardiac ward was not enough to keep up with the inflationary pressures of the time. Eventually she had to advertise for flat-mates.

She was sick of women, and of nurses in particular. She wanted to live with people outside the hospital circle but, after two weeks of interviewing boys looking for a mother to keep house or salacious men who couldn't keep their eyes off her substantial breasts, she despaired of finding anyone suitable. What a relief it was to open the door to a capable-looking bloke like Pete. And Patsy? Well Lou always was a sucker for a damaged soul.

Only later did it she come to understand that the whole Wairua crowd came as part of the deal. Soon the house was full of ragged young people who often did not have the wherewithal to pay the rent. Aussie Joe's old truck dripped oil on the driveway and was always arriving back with more stuff to fill the backyard with a conglomeration of tarpaulin-covered stacks. The hallway was an obstacle course of drums and tea chests.

In September the men went off down the Coromandel to demolish the church and she was left to support Patsy through her final weeks of pregnancy. The one they called Tom Cat had lost no time moving into Big Lou's bed and now she could no longer ignore the fact that she too was pregnant. So she left the house and nursing behind her to follow the Wairua crowd over to the island at the start of December. That first summer they lived in tents and she and Patsy, with Marama, a babe in arms, cooked meals for the men on an open fire and did their washing in the creek.

It was from conversations such as this, when alcohol washed the covering away from fragile roots, that Lou had learnt about the darkness of Patsy's childhood, being the youngest of a large Catholic family. It remained a confidence between them, concealed by the story of how Patsy ran away from her Tauranga home on her sixteenth birthday and hitched to the Coromandel. This she brandished as a testament to her radical spirit. At first an old Maori woman let her live in her shed until the whanau moved her on, not wanting some upstart Pakeha taking advantage of their kuia. From there she drifted down the coast to Thames and found work in a fish-and-chip shop belonging to Pete's parents. Pete found her there when he come home for Christmas from Tauranga where he was serving his boat-building apprenticeship. Ever since he had been her protector – until now it seemed.

Two weeks ago, as they sailed towards Rangitoto she had confessed to Pete that she was pregnant but could not bring herself to have an abortion. He had not taken the news well.

"Scared that Flashy-Britches will find out," Patsy sniffed and threw back her brandy in a single gulp. "Not that it was even necessarily his. It could have been Richie's or that other bloke's."

The sudden movement unsettled the cat. He extended his claws into her knee and his purring veered towards menacing. Patsy stroked him as she continued her story.

Pete had immediately changed course for Auckland and dumped her at the viaduct instead of taking her to Waiheke to spend the night with his sister, Maryanne, as they had planned. Maryanne had still been at school when Patsy worked in the fish-and-chip shop and they had been close friends ever since.

"The last thing he said to me was 'Get rid of it' as he sailed off," said Patsy. "Poor little thing." Her voice broke and she stared up at her crystals arranged above the sink while she quelled her tears.

The shadows trembled as a draught ran over the candles. Lou, who was finishing off a jumper for Gabe, put down her knitting and got up to stoke the fire. Patsy topped up their glasses. Once Lou's needles had resumed their steady rhythm Patsy took a deep breath and continued.

She had stayed with her sister, Belle, while she went through the whole abortion procedure. Belle ran a stall at the Cook Street Markets called *Dragonfare* where she sold crystals, incense, figurines and jewellery, although lately, as the mood of the age changed, she had been moving into bric-a-brac: oddments that she picked up on day-trips into the countryside. She lived with an eclectic group of artisans in an old villa on Ponsonby Road where the front door was always open so people could just wander in off the street on a whim. It was an easy stumble home from the Gluepot and usually Patsy loved staying there, but this time Belle's disapproval had worn her down. The day after the abortion she abandoned Auckland and fled to Waiheke to stay with Maryanne.

And now Maryanne had thrown her out. Patsy had no idea why. She had done nothing wrong – well, apart from coming home late a few times.

"And I was real careful not to wake the baby ... but honestly Lou, such a light sleeper."

The click of Lou's needles continued. She knew that Patsy could not have had an abortion without needing a long, guilt-repressing binge afterwards. Once the brandy was finished, when she judged the time was right, she suggested, once again, that over-indulgence in sex, drugs and rock 'n roll was not doing Patsy any good. And as usual Patsy gave way to tears and said that this time she really did mean to change.

The next morning Patsy had recovered some of her bounce and offered to have Ben and Nick stay on for another few days to give Lou some time to get everything back in order. So Lou, light of heart and with time to spare, decided to visit Kate, who had just taken a tray of Anzac biscuits out of the oven. One coffee stretched into two. Gabe and Melissa were playing 'going to town' out on the deck and begged Kate to let Gabe stay the night.

Kate reassured Lou that she would be happy to have Gabe if only to keep Melissa out of her hair. "You can pick him up when you come down tomorrow."

"Am I coming down tomorrow?" Lou folded her trouser leg over and thrust her foot into her boot. "Oh yeah, that's right, it's benefit day and we're going to have lunch together to discuss the ball. Fuck, I forgot to tell Patsy. Oh well, she'll be up for it."

"No doubt," answered Kate dryly from the doorway. "I've had a few ideas for a floorshow but we'll talk about it tomorrow."

"But I thought Lizzie wanted to do Mouse's song?"

Kate laughed with all the complacency of one who has superior knowledge. "You must be joking. No way would Mouse get up and sing in front of a crowd of people. I'm surprised she even sang to us yesterday. And anyway," she continued as she followed Lou out into the sunlight, "she really isn't much of a singer. I mean ... I don't know what that tune was meant to be but it sounded very flat to me."

The sun was already on its downward slide by the time Lou topped the first rise of the Wairua track and rested by a venerable old puriri tree festooned with a whole community of flaxes, ferns, epiphytes, mosses, fungi, insects and spiders. The tranquility of the bush, dozing in that still winter's afternoon, enveloped her. Everything was swollen with water. Even under the shelter of the big tree a damp chill seeped up from the earth. Over on the next ridge a tui's trilling melody ended in a hiccoughing chuckle. Above Lou, another replied. A warbler's song rose and fell against the syncopated rhythm of the creek below. The fantail that hung out in those parts skipped from branch to branch, twittering happily as it snapped up insects, like a messenger from the Goddess welcoming her home. She perched on the large puriri root that ran along the upper fringe of the track and absorbed the mauri of the land.

She had turned 30 in May. Six months earlier she had marked her Saturn's return – that moment when Saturn returns once more to its position on the natal chart and signals a change in the life journey – by sorting through all her belongings and burning anything that had reminded her of Tom. She had wanted to end the compulsion to go down to the shop every mail day hoping for word from him, to the leap of her heart every time Rose handed her over any vaguely personal-looking letter.

Eight months it had been without a word. He had gone over to Australia to look for work, promising to send for them to join him when he was settled. In May Ben had got a birthday card from him with an Australian postmark but no letter, no money, no address. Lou thought that, for all the comfort it brought Ben, he might as well not have bothered but her will began to waver, She went back to dreaming of his return, yearning for his arms to be around her once more.

The long drought had ended on Saturday night. Even though she woke up alone, she had felt so good that it had been a struggle to keep the post-fuck grin from her face. Fortunately Patsy had been too full of her own concerns to notice but now guilt was eroding Lou's euphoria. It was not only that Patsy called Richie her "toy boy" and that Lou was five years older again. It wasn't that she knew he only slept with her because he had got tired of waiting for Patsy. No, it was about loyalty, which was silly. Patsy usually flitted on from man to man she had drunk her fill. *And after all,* Lou reasoned to herself, *Richie was working his way through the female population like a man with a belt to notch. Why should she not take her turn? But still...*

Now she had to face Aussie Joe. The righteous anger that impelled her to pack the Beast Machine to the gunwales with as much of their stuff as she could fit in around the boys and to take refuge at Patsy's, vowing never to return, was reignited. How dare he demand the attic for himself just because he couldn't afford to return to Oz to work over the winter as he usually did? Why should she and the boys move down into the doss-pit to give him his own space? What about her space in the evenings when the boys were all tucked away? So what if his hut was too cold in the winter? Why should his being a shareholder give him first dibs on where he slept?

Pete's efforts to persuade her to change her mind had not helped. That she had to rely on the fact that she was the mother of Tom's boys to stay in the church stuck in her craw. She had not forgotten that it had been her money that had kept the house in food and rent all those months when they had been preparing to move to the land. They had told her then that the names on the company papers were merely a formality. They were a community, they had said, and should trust one another.

To Patsy, caught in a trough of indecision that compelled her to draw runes from their silken bag every five minutes, Lou's predicament had been a sign that she should sail off with Pete on the next tide. Big Lou would have a place to stay while she decided what she would do and Patsy would have someone to take care of Marama, the ginger cat, the hens and the after-hours exchange while she was away.

"Meant to be," she had sung as she waltzed out the door.

Three weeks later and Lou now realized that she there was nowhere else she could go with three small boys in tow. Death, that potent Tarot card of transformation, had been revealing itself a lot lately but it seemed that an accumulation of past choices had narrowed her life's journey into a deep rut. With a sigh she heaved her pack on to her shoulders and started off down the track.

"Oh Goddess," she prayed, "Give me strength to cope with whatever lies ahead."

She was well armed. She had been twelve when her mother died, leaving her to keep house for her cow cocky father and two younger brothers, and she had quickly discovered that the smell of cooking has a calming affect on men. Unfortunately she had not had enough money left to buy meat but baking is a close second when it comes to managing men. And Patsy had brought her some real coffee back from town, which always goes down a treat.

The sound of a chainsaw ripped through the peaceful afternoon. She had noticed Dutchie's land rover parked at the start of the track but assumed he was visiting Horse Fly. He must have brought his chainsaw over to help out. At least now there would be firewood. She offered up a prayer of thanks to the Goddess.

"If the worst comes to the worst we can always move in with him," she murmured to herself. With a lighter heart she balanced from rock to rock as she crossed the swollen creek and picked her way up the last rise to the church.

Pete had chosen this spot so that he could see the church up there on the hill when he sailed home. He wanted it to stand east/west as he remembered it from his childhood. But everyone else wanted a verandah where they could catch the evening sun so it was rebuilt lying north/south with the arched double doors set into the side of the nave and shaded by a lean-to verandah.

Coming on it like this Lou could almost fancy that a ghostly vicar was still waiting there to welcome his flock. Certainly shades from past summers lurked in the shadows, drinking home brew and passing around joints as they wove intricate webs of Pick 'n' Mix sexual politics and traced high minded visions of 'community' and 'love' in the clouds of marijuana smoke.

"A whole pattern of shades,' Lou thought with a rueful laugh, sighing for the days when the dream was still young.

Horse Fly's dog Grunt and Dutchie's huntaway rushed to meet her with joyous barks, sending the hens scattering every which way. Horse Fly, assiduously plying a hoe over in the garden, gave her cursory wave. Joe had the radio tuned to Hauraki and loud rock music spilt out from the open doors against the background roar of the chainsaw. She stepped up on to the verandah, shrugged off her pack and stood at the doorway, surveying the interior, trying not to breathe in the stench of dead smoke and stale food.

A staircase, leading up into the attic where the children always slept, divided off the doss-pit from the rest of the nave. Here mattresses were piled and bookshelves lined the walls between the windows, full of an eclectic array of books and oddments that had been left there by passers-through. The disassembled chainsaw was laid out on a table beneath the window.

A capacious stone fireplace, where the altar would once have stood, dominated the sanctuary at the opposite end. She viewed with disfavour the fire-blackened, dried-on-rice covered saucepan standing on the hearth and the mattress laid out where the couch and armchairs usually were. It was covered in a tangle of sheets and blankets and surrounded by a confused muddle of cast-off clothes, overflowing ashtrays, dirty dishes and a scatter of paperbacks lying spine-split.

Aussie Joe came through from the vestry with a broom in his hand, his round face split into its usual goofy, lopsided smile. "Ha, you're back," he shouted above the racket. "What've you done with Gabe?"

She was shocked at his appearance: the tangled lumps of dark shoulder-length hair that straggled beneath a woolly hat pulled down to cover his brows, the burgeoning whiskers that, with the heavy bags beneath his eyes, concealed his expression so she could not read whether his welcome was genuine or not, and the clothes that looked as if he had not changed them since she left. His smile ebbed away as he watched her taking in his surroundings.

The sound of the chainsaw eased to a mutter and Annie Lennox, singing *Sweet Dreams are Made of This,* took over the aural space. Lou passed on through to the vestry where higgledy-piggledy piles of dirty dishes littered the bench and table and silt-laden water spluttered from the cold-water tap. A plume of smoke gushed from the stove mingling with a sickly stink of rotting food scraps. The chainsaw's noise intensified once more.

"The water should clear soon," Joe roared from the doorway. "Water's been off since the storm so the dishes have piled up a bit. Hell of a job to fix it, been up and down the creek a dozen times tryin' to untangle the fuckin' line. Taken me all morning. We're out of wood too. Any sign of Pete yet with the new bar? No worries … Dutchie's brought his over and Eddie's here to give him a hand. He and Trev got a pig on Saturday. He's brought us a roast. Good thing you're back. You can give us a hand to get things straight. Only just lit the stove so the water'll be a while yet."

"From the look of that smoke it could've done with a good clean before you started," Lou remarked.

His perpetual smile twisted. "Same old Lou … never satisfied," and he returned to the nave to continue his sweeping.

Lou leant against the cluttered bench. Outside the vestry window Dutchie and Eddie were working together in a fluid dance. Dutchie, large and square, wielded the chainsaw with an easy grace. Eddie, feeding a length of manuka through the cradle to him, dropped the tail end on to the pile and swung out to heft up another length from the stack. The chainsaw's roar receded. While he was waiting Dutchie kicked the pile of firewood he had just cut aside. His heavy work-boots were covered in sawdust.

Once Lou had scraped and stacked up all the dishes, she took the overflowing scrap bucket out to the chook run beside the garden, followed by a swarm of hungry hens, who clucked and squawked at one another as they fought over the choicest scraps.

"Looking good," she called to Horse Fly.

He looked up from the broad beans he was tying back. "Coming on. So the mad bitch is back, is she?"

"Sure is."

Back in the kitchen she began to mix up some scone dough and prepare the roast while she waited for the water to get hot enough for the dishes. When Aussie Joe had finished tidying up his mess she sent him out to the Beast Machine for more of her stuff. By the time he returned the smell of coffee brewing gently at the back of the stove mingled with that of the freshly baked scones she had just taken from the oven before the roast went in. Dutchie, Eddie and Horse Fly were gathered around the table waiting expectantly. Eddie had taken out one of his finest heads and was passing it around so they could smell it appreciatively and compare it with other great heads they had smoked.

Dutchie was moaning on about the McLarens again. Not only was there is no legal access to his land but the McLarens drove their tractor up and down the farm track all the time turning it into a bog. And if he had known that their cattle would be left free to graze every winter and that his ten acres was smack in the middle of their route, well, he would never have bought the land in the first place.

"It's all very well for de old man to say I should fence my whole property," he harangued the others as Lou served the coffee, "but dat's not de case at all. He should be fencing his cattle in. Dat's the legal position. I would have done dem two bastards on Friday night if the udders hadn't pulled me off." He reached for one of the scones that Lou placed in the middle of the table and sat back munching vigorously.

Horse Fly whistled softly to himself.

Eddie licked the paper of the joint he had just rolled, smoothed it down and lit it.

The hot-water cylinder rumbled.

The conversation turned to pig hunting and the genealogy of Trev's latest bitch and went on to range over a number of other dogs and hunting yarns.

After a time Dutchie eased himself up from the table. "Ah well," he said, "Dose cows won't milk themselves."

"You're comin' back for the roast though?" insisted Aussie Joe. "I'll come and help you, if you like. We can bring up the rest of Lou's stuff on the way back."

They went off down the track together. Horse Fly disappeared in the direction of his place over on the other ridge. Eddie stayed to help Lou with the dishes.

"I can't believe little Jesse's a year old already," Big Lou said to him. "Seems like no time since he was a newborn."

"Yep." He worked his way through a fistful of cutlery. "Right little bruiser he is too," he added glancing up at her with a proud parent smile. "We had a bit of a do to celebrate."

"And you had the girls for the weekend too?" she continued.

He sorted out the spoons from the forks to put in the cutlery drawer. "Yeah ... well ... a family occasion, you know. Angel thought his sisters should be there."

"But not Mouse?"

His short laugh was tinged with bitterness. "No point in creating waves. Angel and Mouse, you know ..." He laughed again and shook his head.

They worked away in silence for a while until Eddie looked up from the plate he was drying. "Even then Angel and I had a fucking big blow up. I go hunting to get some fucking pork for the party and she moans because she has to look after the girls. What'd she expect? There's no fucking pleasing her these days."

Lou was applying the pot scrub to a particularly encrusted jar. She could have said something but decided against it.

"She's on to me to move in with her over there," Eddie went on, "but I just need one more year and the house'll be sweet as."

Yeah, and one more dope crop, Lou thought to herself. "Has she weaned Jesse yet?" she asked.

"Nah. That's the real problem, I reckon. He's sucking her dry. That's what she says anyway. I'm going back over there on Wednesday to look after him so she can go over to town for a break."

"That's very noble of you, Eddie," Lou said in mock admiration.

"Ah well, anything for a bit of fucking peace," he shrugged. "I'll get those plans Kate wants done so it won't all be time wasted."

Lou made a start on the pots. He had finished the plates and was well into the mugs before she spoke again. "I saw Mouse on the weekend. She came to the shop with Kate." Her back was to him. She was propping the pots on the end of the stove to dry. "She'd thought up a song ... quite short, but funny in its own way."

Eddie was having trouble finding the best order to hang the mugs from their nails. "Oh yeah?" he said when they were sorted. "Sing it then."

"Oh no," she replied. She wiped down her end of the bench. "Lizzie's putting on a ball on election night and we're going sing it then. I wouldn't want to spoil the surprise."

"Mouse is going to sing it?" scoffed Eddie. "You'll be lucky."

"We'll see. I'm just going to get the veges in and then I'll nip out to the garden for some silver beet. You want to light the lamps while I'm gone?"

Lou lingered in the garden squashing the odd snail she found amongst the rampant weeds. She gathered up a large bunch of silver beet and pulled off some of the rhubarb that was spilling out of the corner by the henhouse to make a crumble for afters. Then she remembered some dandelion wine she had stashed back in the autumn in the remnants of an old shed down an overgrown track through the bush behind the garden. The sun was sinking through a bank of clouds on the horizon, turning everything golden. The greens were piercing in their brightness, the textures of the bark stood out against tangles of creepers. She breathed in the smell of the bush, all leaf mould and growing things, and offered a reverent prayer of thanks to the Goddess.

Lovely, lovely place ... pity about the people.

When she got back the men were clustered around the table in the yellow glow of the Coleman lamp listening intently to the news on 1YA while Horse Fly rolled another joint. When the news came to an end Aussie Joe turned off the radio. The hiss of the lamp filled the silence. Horse Fly lit the joint and handed it to Eddie.

"This Douglas bloke's on to it," observed Aussie Joe. "There's too much government interference in this country. Everywhere you turn there's some fuckin' bullshit standing in your way. Things are much freer in Oz."

"Certainly be good to get out of Piggy's grip," agreed Eddie. "All these wage and price freezes ... import restrictions... even how much money you can take out of the fucking country ... it's holding us back."

When the joint was finished Big Lou got up to make the rhubarb crumble and cook the silver beet while the men continued to jaw away about the election. The roast filled the room with delicious smells that intensified when Big Lou opened the oven to take it out. The boys visibly brightened.

There's nothing, nothing, she thought to herself, *like the smell of meat cooking to set a bloke right.* She popped the crumble in and made the gravy, enjoying the warmth of the room, the subdued light and the jocular company of the men.

It was a lovely meal. The meat fell off the bone, glistening with juices and smelling of pineapple sage and garlic. The potatoes were perfectly crispy on the outside and fluffy in the middle, the pumpkin sweet and the kumara like they were coated in caramel. Lashings of gravy contrasted with the green of the silver beet. Fresh cream from Dutchie set off the crumble a treat and the dandelion wine splashed clear, golden and potent into their glasses.

The boys rolled joint after joint while they vied with one another to keep her entertained well into the night with yarns about hunting, fishing, building and growing dope. Good company, good food, some sticky buds and a bit of liquor ... just another day in Paradise. It almost felt like old times except for the hidden reefs of past nastiness lurking too close to the surface.

The Abysmal

A shard of sunlight through the loft window bounces off the sketchbook propped on my knees. The gentle rhythm of the waves slopping against the rocks halfway down the beach is overlaid by the sound of vehicles changing gear to wind back over the hill. The boat loomed into sight when I was hanging the clothes on the line so there'll be a frenzy of unloading and loading going on over at the wharf. Blithe Spirit yearns to track a line of footsteps over the empty sand but I've been busy all morning getting the shed into a state close to order so I'll be ready to draw.

The girls and I often draw together but when I was in town organizing the DPB someone told me that drawing could be a therapeutic activity. So I bought a set of coloured pencils and this sketchpad solely for my use – the girls are not allowed near them – but it wasn't until Janey started school halfway through May that I had any time to begin.

The ritual starts down at the kitchen table where I draw a frame around the page and sharpen my pencils. Then I retire up here to the loft, lay out the pencils on the window-ledge beside me in the order I plan to use them and smoke a joint while I wait for inspiration. Once the drawing's finished I pin it to the wall at the foot of my mattress so I can look at it when I'm lying up here wasting time. The urge to draw fades once the wall's full, however, which is why I clear it every new moon. An empty wall cries out to be filled and also offers an opportunity to take a new direction.

The best therapy seemed to lie in exploring the limits of this abyss I'm trapped in so I began by working with variations of black, grey, burnt umber, and a slight touch of burnt sienna for contrast, to depict the cliffs surrounding me but last month I started to play with some brighter shades to draw the dragons.

Emerald slime surrounds the bog where High Anxiety wallows with only her closed eyes showing, like two denuded tennis balls. Even though she's always calling me to hide with her it's not a place to linger for Deep Despair lurks below and from there ... no return.

Harshly Critical has magenta eyes and skin seared to terracotta. He stokes a fire in a cave just at the entrance to the only path that would lead me out. Oh how I bask in his heat when it shines on someone else's shame. But it's not long before his focus returns to me and I'm sent scurrying back to cower with High Anxiety again, submerged in a morass of doubt and fear.

I drew Stern Discipline in indigo. He has all the rigidity of a Victorian patriarch, enthroned up on a high ledge where the air is cleaner and the breathing easier. I could enjoy some measure of contentment if I stuck with him, never deviating from my daily routine. But some days I just don't have the energy to get up there and on others I yearn to be free of all his constraints.

All the while, on a needle of rock above me, Blithe Spirit pirouettes in vacant joy. She is festooned with feather boas and leis of plastic flowers so that her slight form is lost in a swirl of violet and emerald, scarlet and lemon, that mingles with her long cadmium yellow hair. Oh how I love dancing in the gloaming with Blithe Spirit, up there where the darkness thins and there's a glimpse of reflected light. But it only lasts for an in-breath. All too soon I lose my footing and tumble down into the swamp once more.

Today, however, I'm going to start in a new direction. I'm going to draw *The Well* and *The Abysmal* from my reading yesterday. My pencils are arranged accordingly: a rainbow, from red through to violet, that peters out into the browns, blacks and greys. To a chorus of High Anxiety's mythering and Harshly Critical's caustic comments, set off by the change of palette and subject matter, I light the remains of the joint I started at morning tea and squint through the smoke at the empty page and the blank wall in front of me.

The Well has been cleaned but no one draws from it. Obviously it's not the bog at the bottom of this abyss then. The king must be clear-minded if good fortune is to be enjoyed by all and who could be clear-minded in this murk? No, the Well may have been cleaned but it lies beyond this desolation.

The Abysmal is water repeated: water flowing downward, filling up every hollow before flowing on until it finally reaches the sea. Downward is not the direction I need to go but the journey is the same: a steady tramp upward from one ledge to another into the light where the Well will be found surrounded by flourishing plants that fill the air with the scents of spring.

I take up pink and a warm grey to depict the rock wall of the Well and lose myself in the contemplation of the light and shadow that is drawing. Ferns and flowering plants grow out of the cracks between two rows of rock that are splattered with orange and silver lichen. Tiny insects live in grasses and moss that grow around the Well, bees work the flowers and butterflies flit above the clear water.

The Well is made up of water above and wood below so the image is of a bamboo pole going down into the well to draw up the water. But no one knows about this well; that it has been cleaned and can be drawn from. So I draw the bamboo pole standing upright against its support. I don't draw the rope that may not go all the way or the jug that may break. No water is drawn from this well. It floats alone in an empty space with nothing to anchor it.

How pleasant it would be to lose yourself in an afternoon snooze, Blithe Spirit suggests. *Nothing you produce can match the perfection of the pictures in your head.*

The shard of light has grown until the whole loft is bathed in somnolent warmth. I slip into a doze and dream of the perfect Well I would draw if I were actually an artist. Further and further down I sink into a world where the hum of insects fills the air that is yellow with sunlight. So much better than my paltry effort with its poorly defined shadows and lack of highlights, its uneven pencil strokes and water that lies on the surface of the page.

Suddenly High Anxiety screws up my stomach like it's a freshly rinsed sheet. My breath is trapped behind my ribs. Voices are intruding on my inner world.

Watch out, they'll see you. They'll know you're lying in bed and not getting on with your day. Hide! Hide!

I straighten out so quickly that the sketchpad slides off the mattress. I sink down below the windowsill. My breath flows softly out. On an in-breath I edge over to the window so I can peek out without being seen.

Melissa and Gabe are churning up the sand, running in circles with their arms out behind them like wings and making high-pitched droning noises. There is a flick of Lilith's tail over by the pohutukawa where she probes under the kikuyu, falling over the clay bank. Kate is standing just below me. She's staring out to sea, maybe watching the clouds piling up on the horizon. A couple of sacks dangle from her hand. She must be going to collect seaweed.

Stern Discipline is rigid with righteousness. *That's what you should be doing, not wasting time drawing. Drawing doesn't feed your children.*

She'll take it all and there'll be none left for you, shrills High Anxiety. *Then you'll never have a garden and your kids will hate you.*

Yeah, because all you ever feed them is rice, adds Harshly Critical.

If my back is pressed hard against the wall I can't be seen from the beach but even so I still feel exposed. I reach down for the sketchpad and start to work quickly, without care, anxious just to finish so I can get down out of the loft and out of sight. The song comes into my mind and I sing it over beneath my breath until it loops around and around in my head. Across the bottom of the page black rocks circle the abyss. The empty space between here and the well is filled with green. I use a tree growing up the side of the page to cover the remaining space: a gnarled old pohutukawa with roots twisting along the top of the cliff and down over the edge. One bough hangs over the well tying the whole picture together. A smudge of blue for the sky and it's finished.

In the excitement of the moment I forget that I'm supposed to remain hidden. I scramble forward to pin this, the first drawing of the new moon cycle, on the wall just as Flash Kate, who has now filled her sacks with seaweed, is leaning back to straighten the cricks out of her spine. She catches sight of me and waves. It would be rude not to wave back.

Let's go down, Blithe Spirit sings out. *It's such a lovely afternoon. You can talk to her about the song.*

And pick up some seaweed while you're there, puts in Stern Discipline.

I'm always nervous about encroaching on Flash Kate's time. I know she never wanted us to move in here, that she only agreed to help me because of Lou.

After I had thrown the porridge at Angel I so needed to escape that I took the girls on a trek over the hill to Wairua to talk it over with Big Lou. I'd got to know her a little when we stayed there last winter and there was no one else to turn to. Instead of the stories and songs we usually divert ourselves with when we're walking I trudged on in silence with the girls trailing along behind. I knew they were upset by what they'd seen but where were the words to justify it? As soon as we reached the church they followed the shouts of the boys down to the creek as if they couldn't wait to get away.

Lou's such a sympathetic soul. She was up in the attic making the boys' beds when I called out to her but she came straight down and took me through to the vestry to put the kettle on. While I sobbed out all my unhappiness she busied herself mixing up a batch of scones so I didn't need to look at her.

"Oh God, I'm such a fuckwit," I ended. "I can't go back and face them after this, I can't." I straightened up and looked around me. "I'll have to leave." A fresh bout of tears overtook me. "But where can I go? Not Orewa. My mother's so ... I'm such a failure. And anyway I don't want to leave the island ... I love it here." I wailed.

While the scones were cooking Lou made a fresh pot of tea and sat down at the table with me. "There's that boatshed below Kate's," she suggested. "She must have the Brody's number. You could give them a call."

"But I've got no money," I cried. "Only the family benefit and that's barely enough to feed us let alone pay rent."

"Well what about the DPB? I can't believe you're not on it already. How long's Eddie been with Angel?"

"Eddie doesn't want to have to pay child support. He thinks it's better if he just buys the girls what they need when he's got work. You know, he picks up the odd bit of building work. And Angel's on the benefit. That keeps us afloat."

A kaka whistled on the pear tree outside then flew off with a screech.

"Gone to tell his mates the pears are ready for plunder," laughed Lou. We talked a bit about the kakas and their taste for fruit.

Lou got up to take the scones from the oven but when she returned she pinned me eyeball-to-eyeball. "You've got to get it sorted, Mouse. Honestly, once it's done you'll wonder why you've left it so long."

"But what if they find out about Angel living with Eddie?" I asked. "Then she'll lose her benefit and ..."

"Why would they?" broke in Lou. "You don't have to tell them that. And anyway so what if they do? Develop a bit of spine, girl. Go back and tell Eddie that you're leaving and that he's got to look after the girls while you go to town to get on the DPB. I've got a bit of money put by you can borrow to see you through and I'm sure Belle'd put you up so you don't need to go back to Orewa. We'll go down this afternoon to see about the boatshed and then you may as well stay the night. It'll be easier to face them tomorrow."

There was a part of me that wished Eddie would beg me to stay so I wouldn't have to move out amongst strangers. That was pure fantasy, of course. He kept his distance while I packed our meagre belongings into four aluminium drums and a couple of boxes and carried them down to the beach ready for Pete to pick up at Easter on his way back from dropping off some building materials further up the coast. Then I left the girls at Fissure Bay and went off to town to organize everything. By the end of April we were settled in here.

Lonely days followed. Everywhere unfamiliar faces pressed in around me. When I had to go to the shop I waited until the tide was low enough to walk around the beach so I could avoid the road and didn't need to talk to anyone. Tracey spent most of the time she wasn't at school down on the beach with Thad, as if she was ashamed of me. On the other hand Janey turned into my shadow and I had to prise her off me to send her to school when the time came. Kate, I hardly saw at all. When she did come down to the beach I stayed in the boatshed hoping she would visit but she never did.

She's got friendlier since Pete sailed off to paint his sister's bathroom. A couple of times she's come out on her deck and yelled down to me to come up for a game of Scrabble and we went to the shop together on Saturday. I wouldn't presume, of course. I always wait to be invited. You never know when the shutters will be slammed shut again. And maybe I'd better make the most of it while I can because when Pete gets back she won't need me any more.

Flash Kate's arranged on the boat-ramp with her back leaning against the shed and one arm resting on the leg bent up in front of her. The other leg dangles over the side of the ramp. She's barefoot and idly picking up pebbles with her frog-like toes and flinging them away. Her toenails are painted an intense shade of pink. From time to time she glances over to where the children are playing horsey on a low hanging bough of the pohutukawa but mostly she is facing out to sea where the boat's wake ripples out across the unruffled sea. Lilith is asleep next to Kate's gumboots that stand by the rock steps, side-by-side with her socks draped over them. She looks up as I come down towards them in my socks because it's too cold to take them off but a bit over-kill to put on my boots.

"Isn't this weather divine," she sighs.

"It's closing in again though." I settle on the lowest step.

"Yeah. It's turning westerly again according to the forecast." Kate continues tossing pebbles … rattle … click … rattle … click. Up on the ridge the trees are swaying in the breeze.

I push Lilith's nose out of my crotch, smooth down her ears and jerk my head to one side to escape a flick of her tongue. She slumps down between us.

The dragons are restless. They roam the confines of their lairs searching for something to hurl at me.

"You looking after Gabe?" I ask.

"Yes, he wanted to stay and it keeps Melissa out of my hair having someone to play with. Patsy's back … finally. Lou was going back up to Wairua so I offered to take Gabe for the night to give her some space to get things set up."

"She'll be glad to get home after all this time."

"Maybe." Kate flicks a glance my way.

The rattle-click continues. I can't think of anything to say that won't upset her. Stern Discipline is concerned that my socks will wear out so I take them off.

Suddenly Flash Kate leaps up, takes a handful of pebbles and flings them out over the beach. "Fuck it must be great to be a man, mustn't it? Just free to go off wherever you like, to have kids and never be tied to them.'

"Men have to work though," I say.

"And we don't?" She glares at me. "The only difference is that their work has some end whereas woman's work goes on forever. We'll never be free to just go off and do our own thing, not until we're too old for it to matter."

What can I do but shrug and wriggle my toes deeper into the shingle? High Anxiety urges me to go back inside where I'll be safe but I can't find a way to leave.

"Still there's compensations to being a mother," I offer.

"Are there? What?"

"Well..." I fold my knees up against my chest and gaze out over the distant ripples at the edge of the sand. "You know ... we get to mould the next generation, I suppose." And I launch into a rave about how the first seven years of a child's life are the formative ones and we get to be with them for five of those. Then I talk about how we develop emotional bonds with our children that sets the groundwork for the relationships they'll have for the rest of their lives.

"And who notices that?" She's standing over me now, fixing me with those crystal eyes.

"Well no one probably. But it's still important. We teach them how to behave correctly and ..." I take a deep breath and stare into the void while I try to find what I am trying to say " ... well acculturate them, I suppose. You know, all that time we spend with them telling them how the world works and being a model for them. Why would you want to trust that to anyone else? And we're closer to our children because of the time we spend with them when they're little."

"And how close are you to your mother, Mouse?"

And I have to tell her how I have failed my mother, who only wanted me to go out into the world and make something of myself like Louisa has. "Whereas me, well I'm dropped out over here," I finish.

"But this is worth something too. We're developing a lifestyle for the future." Kate has sat down on the boat-ramp again and is watching me closely.

"Yeah ... but ... well it takes time, you know ... generations even. We're just laying the groundwork until technology catches up with us."

"Yes, that's what it is, we are ahead of our time," says Kate. She stands up and stretches.

"Yes, ahead of our time" I repeat. "But how do you explain that to like … your parents?"

My how you do go on, smirks Harshly Critical. *Quite the little blabber mouth, aren't we?*

I settle my chin on my knees and sink back down into the swamp. The wind shushes through the trees, full of indefinable longing. Up on the road the school bus stops.

"Jeez, is that the time!" says Flash Kate. "I'd better head back up."

She calls over for Melissa and Gabe to come and pulls on her socks and gumboots. The children's cries sail on the wind. They bounce higher on the bough as if they haven't even heard. Eventually she has to go over to give them a hurry-on. Once she's herded them over she glances at the bags of seaweed.

"Say, would you be a sweetie and carry one of these sacks up for me tomorrow morning?" she asks. "I can't take them both now with the children. You're coming to lunch tomorrow at Patsy's, aren't you? I want to ring Pete so I'll probably go around as early as possible, say about half-nine?"

"Um, okay." I'm still hunched over my knees on the bottom step.

"Don't worry about the floorshow," she says with an encouraging smile. "No one's expecting you to sing the song. I'll think of something we can do."

"Um, yeah, ok," I reply.

"See you then." She swings a sack of seaweed on to her shoulder and guides the two children ahead of her through the flax.

High Anxiety lolls on the surface of her swamp. Her eyes are open and she gazes up at the precipice high above where Blithe Spirit's face is hidden beneath a curtain of mousey hair. I wonder why I've never noticed before how tatty her boas are and the gaudiness of her plastic lei.

Stern Discipline urges me inside, reminding me about the clothes on the line and the shortness of the day.

The dark walls of the abyss press in on me, gleaming in a ghastly firelight as flames roar out of Harshly Critical's cave. *What's wrong with you? It's not like they were ever going to do that simple-minded song anyway.*

Benefit Day

On Tuesday morning Patsy Dervish was enjoying a fresh-brewed coffee and a cigarette while she contemplated her day. The light from the window was dampened by thick drizzle. Sacks of flour, sugar, rice, milk powder, potatoes and onions, and two cartons of groceries seemed to grow out of the settee and merge with the three black-plastic rubbish bags of treasure she had gathered on her travels. Paul – such a sweetie – had taken an extra trip to the wharf yesterday just to bring it all around for her. So ... unpacking ... dishes ... the wine needed bottling too. Her promise to Big Lou was just a vague memory now and anyway, why waste all that feijoa, sugar and effort? Not to mention the three-dozen home-brews she had put down before she went away. She wondered where Richie was.

Now she was left alone with the domestic round, the sorrows she had tried to put behind her came swirling to the surface once more. She would have done it if only Pete had reacted differently – would have brought another soul into this over-crowded world. But the thought of doing everything that comes after, alone and unsupported, had wilted her confidence. Patsy firmly believed that Marama only survived her infant years because Lou had been there to guide her through them. And the thought of having two young souls dependent on her was just ... well it was beyond her. It was as simple as that.

What a fine dream Pete had spun her that first summer when they went sailing off the Coromandel during her time away from the fish and chip shop. He would talk to her about how they would get a group of people together, pool their money, buy some land and find a new way of living that was at one with the planet. Despite their difficulties – her brothers' probing fingers, the cattiness of her sisters and the drunken neglect of her parents – she missed her family in a rose-coloured-spectacles kind of way so it was easy to be swept up by his enthusiasm. She believed then ... everyone in the company believed that they really could change the world.

What was all that now but a wisp of summer cloud drifting away on a breeze? Any lingering illusion that Wairua was a community that would take care of their own had fallen apart in the face of Pete's anger. He might fall into bed with her at the end of a drunken night at the club, when Kate had thrown him out yet again. Then it was just like old times. But how easily she was discarded once Kate had enticed him back again. Patsy knew that Kate would get her own way in the end. Once her house was built he would move in with her up on the hill looking over towards the wharf where he would be closer to his boat. Who would be left at Wairua then? Just a couple of lonely old bachelors. Because Lou was not going to stay. Patsy was sure of that.

Big Lou loomed through the door at just after nine. Patsy had put on *Private Dancer,* the new tape she brought in town, and was channeling all her anger through Tina's raunchy voice – bellowing out, "what's love got to do, got to do with it?" as she pranced between the table and the pantry, unpacking the groceries.

"I forgot to tell you. Everyone's coming for lunch today. Lizzie's putting on a ball," Lou shouted above Patsy's discordant singing.

Patsy finished the dance move she was executing – a leap up on to a chair and a reach to deposit a block of fig meat on to the highest shelf out of the reach of children. She moved across to the tape deck to turn down the volume. "The ball? Yep, already know. Lizzie told me. She's coming over as soon as Paul's back from feeding Reuben's animals.

"You're early. All good up home?"

"Yeah, it's all fine." Lou propped her pack on a chair and took a plastic bag out of her pack. She waved it in Patsy's direction. "Look, I've brought a pork bone down to make soup for lunch. Eddie and Trev got a pig on Saturday and Eddie dropped in with a roast." She bent down to stroke the cat, who had been enticed by the smell of meat to leave his armchair and come over to wind around her legs.

"Brilliant," Patsy, still moving to the muted music, plucked some almonds and brazil nuts out of a carton, leapt on to the chair again and threw them in with the fig meat.

"You want to do the dishes while I finish the unpacking? Then we'll have a cuppa before we go."

Rattles and clangs signalled Lou's displeasure. She had left Wairua early, in the hopes that the men would do the dishes in her absence, and Patsy, while continuing her dance, had to burrow deep into her aggrieved silence with bright questioning before she recovered her equilibrium.

Once the doings up at Wairua had been dealt with and Aussie Joe's state of mind discussed, the conversation turned to the lunch and on to Mouse.

"Why's she coming?" Patsy asked. "She hardly says boo to anyone, doesn't even say hi when she sees you in the shop." She stacked the lentils next to the split peas on the next shelf and turned back to the carton for the sunflower seeds.

Lou told her how Mouse had come to the shop with Kate on Saturday and how Eddie had taken the girls up to Angel's for Jesse's first birthday party.

"And she didn't go? See she's such a piker," cried Patsy who would never miss a party, even if she were not invited.

So Lou told her what Eddie had had to say about that. Their voices bounced around the kitchen as they parried back and forth about the ethics around ownership of another person. Patsy held that no one owned anyone else. If Eddie and Angel were together Mouse should just accept that and move on. But Lou said that it was not so easy to leave behind a childhood friend and someone you were married to as well.

"See you've never really loved anyone, Pasty. You always flit on before you've had time to care. When you've lived with someone for years and had kids with them ... well, it hurts. And there's your children's pain too. That's even harder to bear." The porridge pot came in for sustained scrubbing. "Anyway, I quite like Mouse," she continued. "She sung us this real fun song on Saturday. That's what gave Lizzie the idea of doing a floor show at the ball."

Patsy sashayed out to the porch with the empty cartons and came back to start stowing the sacks of flour and sugar into bins below the shelves in the pantry. "And that's what we're going to sing?"

"Well, Kate doesn't think Mouse'll go through with it. It's not really long enough either ... maybe she'll think up some more words but ... Kate's going to come up with something. She took dancing lessons as a child, you know." They exchanged a glance and Patsy sniggered.

"So Mouse's song, what is it? Some maudlin dirge about spurned love?" she asked through an in-held breath as she hoisted the milk powder sack into a bin and forced it closed.

Once the bench was clear Lou started chopping up some onions for the soup stock. "Not at all. It's about skipping through the trees leaving dishes undone and beds unmade."

"Hah, right on! I can relate to that. Yeah, that'd be better than some rehashed love song from the other side of the world. Still, Kate's right ... much as I hate to agree with her ... Mouse'd probably pike out at the last minute."

Patsy stood back and looked with satisfaction at her well-stocked shelves before she closed the double doors. The pantry was the envy of all her friends who mostly kept their stores in drums or on shelves covered with ragged curtains. She turned to stoke the fire and shift the kettle over the heat.

"Now me, I'm completely done with love. It's abstinence for me from now on," she announced.

"Yeah, well, we'll see how that goes," Lou laughed. "I'll just duck out to the garden for a few herbs."

Patsy carefully positioned two mugs on the table so their handles pointing outward like ears. "You seen anything of Richie?" she asked.

Lou remained at the stove with her back to her. The stock came in for a lot of attention. She moved the bone around and poked the herbs and onions under the water in the stockpot with a wooden spoon. "Yeah he's been around. He was playing Scrabble with Lizzie and Rose on Thursday. That's when she decided about the ball."

"Scrabble? Fuck, he's keen. So slow. And Lizzie's goes right off if you put a word down she doesn't thinks good enough."

"Actually I'm getting quite into it now. I got a seven letter word the other day ... 'bouquet' with the ..."

"Yeah, yeah, fucking groovy." The spoon rattled against the sides of the jar as Patsy mixed up more milk.

"If Richie's so keen," she burst out, "how come he's been down here playing Scrabble with Lizzie all this time and now I'm back he hasn't been near the place?"

"Yeah, well ... he was here on Saturday looking for you but ... you know ... surf's up over the other side." Lou banged down the lid on the stockpot and turned to face her. "Anyway, what does it matter if you're practicing abstinence?" she scoffed.

The tape had long since come to an end. Outside the window there was a ping ... ping ... ... ping ... ping of water dripping off the spouting on to something metal. A slight breeze was breaking up the cloud revealing small gaps of blue sky. Patsy gave the teapot a cursory twirl and poured the tea.

"Yeah, I suppose you're right," she sighed. "Come on, let's have this tea. Rose should be over the worst of the school rush by now."

If anyone had the pulse of the community it was Rose. She had presided over the post office for so long that she was now a fixture, her vast bulk wedged between the counter and the exchange behind her as she glared at her customers down the curve of her predatory nose. From here she kept a finger in many pies in the community – the Fishing Club, Women's Division, the Maori Women's Welfare League, not to mention her own extensive whanau.

The busiest mornings were Mondays and Fridays when the Sea Bee brought in the mail. People always saved up their other post office business to do at the same time so it was a slow-moving queue. A lot of information was bandied about and absorbed by Rose. Not that she was inclined to gossip herself. Hers was a deep sea that rarely revealed its secrets.

Benefit day, every second Tuesday, had a ferment all of its own.

The solo mothers with school-age children often arrived as soon as they had dropped their children off at school. Others came later, when they had finished the morning chores. Some of the women had not spoken to anyone other than their children for days so there was much female laughter accompanied by the shrieks of preschool children.

Rose, who counted solo mothers as less than nothing, gathered up their bankbooks in batches and rang through to the city branch to update them. Mouse was thoroughly alarmed by her and even Patsy, who tried to disarm her with a bright 'kia ora', seldom elicited even the suggestion of a smile. To Lizzie, however, she was like an aunt, a longtime friend of Lizzie's mother who remembered her as a babe-in-arms.

This particular Tuesday Patsy and Lou found Lizzie, who had been at the shop from early morning so the shelves would be restocked before the women arrived, taking advantage of a lull to have a well-earned coffee.

"Paul said he would be back around one so I can come over for lunch," she told them. "Although I'm not holding my breath." She used the excuse of straightening up the sweet jars to take a look around the shop at what her customers were doing.

"All this effort to row over to Reuben's place when he could just as easily take the van," she muttered. "Makes me wonder if he's got his eye on someone else."

Patsy, always keen to hear a morsel of gossip, waited eagerly for Lizzie to go on but Lizzie only glared darkly at the back of the shop and turned away to serve someone else.

Flash Kate guided Melissa and Gabe out of the post office and threaded her way through the shelves towards them. Gabe ran ahead and threw himself at Lou who swung him up to give him a big cuddle while Kate gave a report on his wellbeing. Then Kate turned to survey Patsy as if she was a map from which a story could be drawn if she only knew the code. "So you're back, are you? We all thought you'd done a runner."

Patsy Dervish was intently turning over the frozen lumps of meat in the freezer. "Ah well ... one thing and another, you know ... time just got out of hand."

"I'm waiting to get through to Pete and there are still five people ahead of me," Kate said.

Patsy looked up at Flash Kate, a wide smile digging deep into her cheeks. "Oh well, that wild Waiheke scene, you know, it's hard to leave once you're caught up in it. I doubt Pete'll even be back for the election he's having so much fun."

Kate had taken a can of tomatoes from the shelf. Her grip on it tightened as if she would like to hurl it at Patsy.

Lou cleared her throat. She put Gabe down and took a piece of toilet paper out if her cardigan pocket to wipe the snot from his nose.

"We're heading back as soon as Rose's finished with our books. I'll take Melissa if you like," she offered.

Kate set the can down on the counter as if it were a precious icon.

"Oh would you? That would be so good. You'd like to go with Gabe, wouldn't you sweetie?" She bent down to Melissa who squirmed and clung on to her leg until Lou suggested they could go down to the creek to play boats and gather some watercress.

"We'll buy the port and you can fix us up later," Patsy said to Kate, ignoring the heavy-browed look Lou cast at her.

"You had better not start it until I get there then," Kate replied.

Patsy looked over at Mouse who was hovering at the back of the shop. "You in too?"

"Yeah ... I guess so," she answered.

"I'll wait and come with Kate," she continued, her words bumbling over one another. "I've ..." Her head shrunk back between her hunched shoulders. "... I've got some stuff to do."

Lou took the children to gather watercress while Patsy chopped up the vegetables for the soup and baked some bread. When Lou returned there was still no sign of the other two so Patsy gave the children the cartons to play with in the passageway.

Finally Kate arrived, full of apologies for the delay but in good spirits because she had finally got through to Pete. He was doing some work on a boat down at the causeway and would not be back until the following week, which was disappointing but at least they had got to talk. She put a cake tin and some cream cheese on the bench and moved over to warm herself beside the stove before she mixed up some icing. "Mmm, something smells nice. Is that pork?"

"Yeah, Eddie and Trev got a pig on Saturday. We had roast up at Wairua last night," boasted Lou.

"He sent us some chops home with the girls," put in Mouse. She had followed Kate in, hid a plate of dry griddle scones spread with a faint smear of honey on the bench behind the port and edged into the chair nearest the door.

"Oh yes, It was Jesse's first birthday party, wasn't it? I hear Eddie had the girls for the weekend." Patsy leapt up and headed for the bench.

"Port, everyone?"

"They spent the whole of Saturday pig hunting," Lou told them while Patsy poured everyone a drink. "Angel's really pissed off, although I suppose she was happy enough with the pork. She's making him look after Jesse for a week while she takes a break in town."

"It's about time she weaned Jesse," declared Kate. "I thought she looked run-ragged at play-centre last week."

Mouse shifted in her chair and began circling the top of her glass with her finger.

"He reckons he'll do your plans while he's at it, Kate," Lou went on. "He obviously doesn't have a clue how much time looking after a one-year-old can take up."

"Ah all those ladies up there'll be falling over each other to help him out," Patsy scoffed. "You know how it is. They'll treat him like he's a fucking hero just because he's looking after his kid for a change."

A thump from the passageway was followed by a shriek. Melissa fell through the door as soon as it was opened and ran into Kate's arms.

Gabe sat stolidly in one carton with the other one held firmly in his chubby fist. His moon face was dark with defiance. "I needed a dinghy," he said.

Melissa only calmed down when Patsy remembered something she had brought her back from town. She searched through her rubbish bags, a smirk playing the corners of her mouth, and produced a fur stole, a fox biting its tail. Its glittering eyes scared Melissa into silence. Lou laughed uneasily. Even Mouse looked up from her reverie. Kate was strident with disgust. So much so that Patsy was able to coax Melissa, who opposed her mother at every turn, into having it draped over her shoulders.

There is something about a fur that bestows nobility on the wearer. Melissa's tiny frame straightened and her nose pointed skyward as she swanned past Gabe, who had followed her into the kitchen with the cartons still firmly in his grasp. He gazed at the fur with an envy that was only slightly mollified by a tweed sports jacket Patsy found for him.

Kate glowered from the bench where she was putting the final touches to the icing. A spirited debate sprung up between them over the appropriateness of wearing the skins of dead animals. Patsy declared that there was nothing wrong with the stole because the fox had been killed long before anyone saw anything wrong with wearing fur. Kate contended that a dead animal was still a dead animal. She vowed to steal it away once Melissa had fallen asleep and destroy it. Melissa fell into another paroxysm of weeping until Kate promised solemnly not to do any such thing and made the two children a Milo to keep them going until lunch was ready.

However, Patsy was now on a roll. She poked amongst her treasures to find presents for them all. Lou, who hardly ever found anything to fit her in op shops, was delighted with the long flowing velvet dress with the embroidered bodice Patsy had discovered at a garage sale on Waiheke. She shed her corduroys and jumper and tried it on, moving this way and that before the kitchen window to catch the best reflection. Kate received a silk shawl from a K. Road op shop with cold grace but showed more interest in a stack of second-hand books Patsy had brought back to circulate. She chose two, *The Mists of Avalon* and *The Thorn Birds,* and stowed them away in her pack. Meanwhile the children, delighted with a chance to play dress-up, were throwing dresses, jackets, jumpers and trousers around with joyous abandon.

"Enough!" Patsy shouted. "Look at that mess! You're going to have to help me put it all back again now." She looked over at Mouse who sat slouched in her chair as if she had been swallowed.

"And Mouse," Patsy went on. "I knew I would find someone for this. It's too long for me but it was too good to pass up."

Mouse looked up hopefully but shook her head and tried to retreat into herself again when she saw the red dress Patsy was holding up.

"But you'd look so good in it," Patsy enticed her. "Red is definitely a colour for you," she went on, "you know, for parties."

"I'd never wear it," replied Mouse. Her hands were hidden under her thighs. "Honestly, I never wear stuff like that."

"Nonsense. It'll be just the thing for the ball," said Flash Kate.

"Why don't you try it on to see how it looks?" suggested Big Lou.

So Mouse was persuaded to shed her over-sized trousers, bush singlet, flannel shirt and t-shirt. She pulled the slinky red dress over her head and smoothed it down. It clung to her small waist and firm buttocks then flared out to reveal shapely, although of course unshaven, legs.

The other ladies viewed her thoughtfully.

"Turn around," ordered Kate. "She needs some heels," she mused. "I don't suppose you have any heels?"

Mouse shook her head and began to pull the dress off again.

"No wait." Patsy sorted through the pile again. "Here, what about these? Will they fit you?"

"I couldn't wear those," Mouse muttered, looking at the black high-heeled shoes Patsy had found. "I haven't worn heels in years. I'd fall over."

"Course you can. It'll just take a bit of practice," laughed Lou. "Go on, give them a go."

"Yes, you definitely need practice," Kate pronounced after Mouse had teetered around the kitchen. "Still your legs are your best feature and those shoes really show them off. I could lend you some black tights to go with them, if you like. And you need a bra. Do you have a bra?"

"Somewhere." Mouse, swirling around, craning to catch her reflection.

"I suppose I could take them," she said.

"Thank you," she added as an after-thought as she bundled them into her backpack.

They had just given up waiting for Lizzie and sat down for lunch when she came breezing in on a draught of moist air. "Paul's only just arrived back," she said collapsing into the chair beside Lou and tossing a packet of chocolate biscuits on the table. "I didn't have time to bake so I brought these. No skipping through the trees for me, I'm afraid."

"Right on time," replied Patsy. "We're about to start. You want soup? Port?"

Over soup Patsy regaled them with tales from her travels until Lizzie broke in and said she did not have much time left so they needed to get on. She reported on the progress so far. Rose had talked to the Fishing Club committee and they were happy to free up the hall for that night and let them use their liquor license so long as there was a 50c cover charge for generator use and the like. Paul would have the invitations printing up in time for one to go out to everyone on the mailing list and Rose would have a pile on the counter to give out to anyone who missed out.

"And I've decided to make it a Fantasy Ball," Lizzie told Kate, "seeing as you want to have a theme. That gives everyone plenty of scope in finding costumes."

Kate inclined her head. "Yes...Yes that could work."

"And no kids. This is an adult affair." Lizzie said in a not-to-be-gainsaid voice.

"But what're we to do with our kids?" exclaimed Patsy.

"Well you'll just have to get a babysitter. There's plenty of teenagers around looking to make some extra money."

"That's just bullshit!" exclaimed Patsy. "Everyone'll be looking for babysitters and it's all just added expense."

"I can't see how it matters," sniffed Lizzie. "They could all stay the night here, have a little party of their own and we could share the cost. The teenagers are always hanging around the shop. I'll ask around."

"I think it's a good idea," said Kate. "It is not often we have a chance go out without the kids."

Patsy got up to brew some coffee while Kate and Lou settled the little ones on the settee with some books for their afternoon rest. Lizzie and Mouse cleared the table. When all was ready Kate sliced the carrot cake and handed it around.

"So have you thought any more about the floorshow?" Lizzie asked Mouse.

Mouse glanced around at them. "Well, only that little song." Her voice was so soft it could hardly be heard above the chatter of the children.

Kate began sharing her ideas but was interrupted by Patsy. "I thought we were doing Mouse's song?" She turned to Lou. "Isn't that what you said?"

Big Lou looked over at Mouse who was fingering the moist interior of the carrot cake.

"My song ..." Mouse swallowed. Her finger traced a line along the edge of the table. "It's not that long and ... probably Kate's idea would be better."

"No. We want to do your song," Lizzie leaned past Lou and looked up into Mouse's downcast eyes. "Something original, you know? Have you heard it?" she turned to Patsy. "It's really good."

Mouse spread her fingers out on the edge of the table.

Kate caught Lou's eye and raised her eyebrows in a what-did-I-tell-you way. She tasted her coffee. "Ah, what a treat, real coffee," she said to Patsy.

But Patsy was staring down the table at Mouse. "Why don't you sing it through so at least I know what we're missing out on," she suggested.

"Yes, come on, Mouse," said Lizzie. "We'll sing it with you."

The collective eyes of the other ladies remained fixed on Mouse until she finally relented. Her hands slid down into her lap and she focused her eyes on a tea towel hanging to dry above the stove. As she began the song the others joined in, waving their coffee mugs in time with the beat.

"Well, we skip though the trees
With the greatest of ease,
First on our bottoms,

And then on our knees.
The dishes aren't done
And the beds are unmade,
And all life is,
Is a pattern of shades."

"Yeah," said Patsy when the song came to an end. "I like it. It's too short though. What about some verses to go with it?"

Mouse lifted her mug to her lips and sipped at her coffee. She looked around the table at the other women: Patsy Dervish and Lizzie with their encouraging smiles, Big Lou full of comfort, and Flash Kate, a slight sneer twisting her lip to one side. She shrugged.

"That's all there is. It ... it just came to me in the night ... like ... sort of ... like a gift from God," she babbled.

"God?" Kate drew back to take Mouse in more fully. "What God? Surely you don't mean the Heavenly Father?"

Patsy stretched out and scooped a dollop of icing off the remaining carrot cake. "Hey listen honey," she remarked, sucking the icing off her finger. "I have an intimate knowledge of God and I'm pretty sure He doesn't hold with undone dishes and unmade beds."

"It was a gift from the Earth Mother maybe," put in Lou softly. "The Goddess."

Mouse gulped down some more coffee. "Yeah, I suppose." Her eyes are back on the tea towel as she searched for words to explain her cosmology. "This thing of God having a gender... I think that's a wrong way of looking at it. Heavenly Father, Goddess ... either way it excludes half the population. God's more like a ... an underlying force, maybe ... that keeps everything in a kind of ... harmonious balance. You know, something that's in everything, that ties it all together."

"That's not God though," burst out Flash Kate. "That's just natural forces. Really Mouse, that doesn't make any sense. A gift implies a giver, a person to give the gift. Forces don't give gifts. They just are."

"It doesn't matter," said Lizzie impatiently. "I'll have to get back now. Shall we catch up again after the shop shuts on Saturday? If this

God has sent you any more gifts by then we'll do your song. Otherwise we'll go with what Kate can come up with. Or we could just forget the whole thing. There's not a lot of time left."

Limitation

Janey doesn't want to go to school. She clings to me, sobbing, as I cajole and threaten. What would I do with her all day if she stayed at home?

It'll take up all your precious time. High Anxiety's agitated pupils buzz like blowflies.

Harshly Critical has been steadily stoking his fire ever since I got back from the lunch yesterday and now has further fuel to add. *Yeah, your precious time,* he sneers, *even though the poor kid's miserable at school.*

But Stern Discipline warns me not to give in or she'll never learn to get on in the world.

Yeah, you wouldn't want her to turn out like you, adds Harshly Critical.

Tracey stands by the table, yawning in a fake, mocking way. "Well are you coming or not," she snaps. "We'll miss the bus if you don't hurry."

"Honey, it'll get better, I promise," I croon, pushing Janey from me and straightening up the backpack on those impossibly frail shoulders. "You could at least be kind to her," I say to Tracey. "She depends on you."

Tracey's eyes sweep over us. She glares at me. "I had to go through this. You didn't hear me crying to be kept at home. And I was at Orewa ... a way bigger school than this. No wonder she gets picked on. She's such a crybaby."

"Well, I hope you look after her," I venture.

"Come on Janey, let's go." Tracey grabs her arm. "The bus'll be here soon." She hurries her out the door into a thick fog that fills the valley.

Back in the loft with my coffee and joint I gaze at my drawing of *The Well*. If there are verses at the bottom of this well I have no way of retrieving them, down here in the abyss, with my mind as befogged as the air outside. The drawing has obvious flaws that I'd like to correct but I've already moved on. This morning I counted out the sticks by candlelight, asking once more about the song.

> *Treading – He treads on the tail of the tiger.*
> *It does not bite the man.*

There're two moving lines. The fourth line talks about caution and circumspection leading ultimately to good fortune. The sixth – even better – advises me to look to my conduct and weigh the favourable signs. It promises supreme good fortune.

Flames billow from Harshly Critical's cave. *What favourable signs?* he badgers. *They'll never sing your song. That about it being too short was just an excuse.* He drives me back ... down ... down into the bog.

High Anxiety draws me even further down, below the surface, my genitals in her tight grasp. *It's just as well. That's what it means about caution and circumspection. If you're careful they'll forget all about this song. Then supreme success will come. Supreme success will be you being left in peace and not making a fool of yourself.*

The fog presses against the window, stifling any sound from the outside world. I suck at the joint until it's well alight then lie back and stare up at the rafters. Smoke trickles out of my mouth and drifts up to mingle with the waves of corrugated iron retreating into the gloom.

Supreme success, gloats Blythe Spirit. *We're on a roll with this one.*

I drift up to join her in a dream about what supreme success could mean ... the adulation of the crowd ... the admiration of my friends ... and love ... so delightful.

Stern Discipline jerks me down from these airy heights. *What about all that mess? You'll need to get that tidied up if there's to be any supreme success,* he grumps.

I send one foot out from beneath the covers on an exploratory mission but withdraw it again. It's probably warmer outside than in this dank shed.

The second hexagram was *Limitation*.

Galling limitation must not be entered into, trills Blythe Spirit. *Let's go fishing.*

By the time I'm organized the tide's nearly full so I have to leap over a crevice between two shelves of rock to get out to the point. There, clusters of crabs cling to the walls. I stab one and stash it in my fishing sack. Out on the point at my usual spot, I quarter it, attach one bit to my hook and fling it way out into the deep pool beneath me. Once I've secured the line to a rock I make myself comfortable on a ledge. I am submerged in the fog. The only sound is the waves sucking softly at the rocks beneath me. I could be the only person left on the planet ... alone in blissful solitude.

Apart from Harshly Critical who's blowing on his dying embers. *Janey's like she is because of you,* he hisses. *You, who can't even step outside your door without your guts tying themselves in knots.*

I light up the joint I brought with me. My fingers are so damp it takes three matches to get it going but soon the smoke stretches my lungs to capacity.

The song, the song, sings Blythe Spirit on the out-breath. *Singing the song will show her that there's nothing to be feared.*

But High Anxiety knows I don't really want to leave the concealing swamp. *Forget about the song.* She beckons me down to where it's safe. *Caution and circumspection means not putting yourself in positions where you're bound to fail.*

Harshly Critical lays some brush on top of the glowing embers, reminding me of the scones I'd made for the lunch yesterday. I'd even spread the last of our honey on them. *So unappetizing! They didn't even take them off the bench where you left them. I bet Patsy's fed them to her chooks this morning. Not even those boys would've eaten them ... not like Kate's lovely carrot cake.* His voice infiltrates my bones.

The ladies loved the song though, pleads Blythe Spirit. *They really want you to do it.*

But the brush has caught now and Harshly Critical feeds on a scatter of twigs. *And all that about God? What was all that about?*

I hide my head on my knees, making myself as small as possibly.

High Anxiety crumples up my entrails. *Hide away until they've forgotten it,* she suggests. *They won't miss you.*

Droplets of water bead on my Swanni, dampening the joint. I stash it in my pocket, shift around to ease the points of pressure and consider the question of God. What about Flash Kate's challenge? Does a gift imply a giver? How can the song be a gift from God if there's nobody to do the giving? Strands of kelp swell up and down with the movement of the tide. *The Tao of Physics* wafts through the marijuana haze.

Matter can be viewed as either particles or waves ... apparently two separate concepts. The current that forms the waves of the sea is distinct from the water itself for the water doesn't travel with the current. It merely moves in circles as the current passes through. This is how matter appears to physicists. It's a field of possible particles, in constant flux: changing their composition, their charge from positive to negative and back, splitting into quite different particles and then joining up, to split again. The rocks beneath me, the sea ... even me, my own body ... are patterns of energy whose attractive force holds a particular form for a time and then disintegrates to take on a new one. The hexagram from an *I Ching* reading plucks a configuration of light and shade from the changing flow of reality. This is how it's similar to physicists' conception of matter, except that physicists deal only with what can be measured, whereas the *I Ching* represents the hidden, spiritual aspect of reality.

That doesn't explain anything, mocks Harshly Critical. *How can a pattern of light and shade give anything to anyone?*

But the currents of the sea do throw up gifts from time to time – a nautilus shell, perhaps, or a peg for the clothesline. Could the changing flow of energy not throw up a gift into my mind?

I pull in my line. The bait was nibbled away while I was thinking. I bait up again and cast the line back into the slow swirl of the sea.

Harshly Critical's fire blazes up. *There is no gift from God,* he exclaims. *The song was just a random event. Nothing will follow. You're too stupid to think up any verses.*

His voice echoes up the looming walls of the abyss, up even to where Blythe Spirit crouches on her precipice, her feather boa dangling from one hand.

High Anxiety closes her eyes and submerges with a contented sigh.

Only the attentive eye notices the gifts of the sea ... like picking up a nautilus shell as you pass ... or realising that the well has been cleaned. The gift is lying there waiting to be discovered if only I could leave the dragons behind and open my mind.

What about Eddie looking after Jesse for a whole week so Angel can go to town, breaks in Harshly Critical sulkily. He lays a larger branch on the bed of embers he has built up. *Even when he does take your girls he doesn't spend any time with them ... just leaves them with her.*

The fog presses in around me. I shift position again and try to relight the joint. After a couple of drags smoke floods down my throat.

Blythe Spirit gives the boa an exploratory twirl. *Richie was real nice to you,* she remembers. *He likes the song.*

Richie arrived after I'd made such a fool of myself talking about God like that. High Anxiety was urging me to leave but I couldn't find the right moment. Big Lou had got up to see to the children so Richie took her seat across from me and straight off asked me about the song . He was so enthusiastic about it that even Flash Kate started thinking it might be a good idea.

He likes you. He likes you. Blythe Spirit starts spinning around in a kaleidoscope of colour.

Crap, snaps Harshly Critical. He levers the branch up to let the air get in underneath. Flames flare up. *What on earth would he see in you, who can't even make a scone that other people might want to eat?*

Richie's attention so unnerved High Anxiety that I had to leave. Flash Kate made a big thing about how school would be out soon and the kids could stay around and play for a while but Big Lou said she needed to head off too and insisted on giving me a lift even though I wanted to walk. And then she barely said anything as we drove along and snapped at Gabe, who was fidgeting between us. She obviously doesn't like the song.

Bite! calls Stern Discipline. *Pay attention please.*

There's a nibble on the line, faint at first and then with increasing urgency, so that all I can think about is fish. I haul up a good-sized snapper, enough to feed us for tonight and make some stock for soup tomorrow.

Wow, rejoices Blythe Spirit. *Pork chops on Sunday night, mince last night, fish tonight … it doesn't get much better than this!*

I'm heading back with my catch when a putt-putt-putt cuts through the thinning mist. I pause astride two rocks to listen. The motor cuts out. An anchor chain rattles.

It's Paul. It's Paul, cries Blythe Spirit, frolicking madly.

With a motor? Hardly, snarls Harshly Critical.

Visitors, anyway, Blythe Spirit exults … *someone to show your fish to. Better hurry or you'll miss them.*

I bound back across the rocks until I reach the boat ramp where Old Tom's hauling up his dinghy.

"Look, I got a fish." I pull the fish out of my fishing sack and hold it up for his inspection.

He inclines his head, turns to stow the oars and lifts a machete out of the bow. He'd promised to drop it off last time I was chatting to him over at the wharf.

"You get that green-weed cleared away," he says, nodding at the green-weed spreading down the slope behind the shed, "and you could have a fair-sized garden there."

While I make a cuppa he cleans and fillets the fish for me. Over tea he tells me about how he ran away to sea at the age of fifteen and spent the summer working as a bellboy, cruising the Pacific. He's such an interesting old guy. I love listening to his yarns so I agree to go back with him to get some vegetables.

Old Tom lives over by the wharf in a one-roomed shack in front of a double skyline garage where he keeps all his tools and machinery. He insists I come in for a drink so I perch on a wooden chair at a red Formica table that wobbles when I lean on it. Beyond Old Tom I can see a single bed, tidily made, taking up the back wall. A sink-bench runs along the other wall beneath some shelves holding a few plates, cups and glasses. A primus stove stands on the bench next to a meat-safe. There is a place for everything and everything in its place but there's a ripe smell to it: fish, fossil fuels, stale urine, compost. So I refuse his offer of food, even though I haven't eaten since breakfast and am quite hungry. He takes down two meat-paste jars – those ones with wide mouths patterned with vertical ridges – and fills them to the rim with OPG.

We plunge straight into discussing the political situation. I'm running my finger up and down the ridges of my jar while he tells me why he's going to vote Social Credit. He's a great believer in Bruce Beetham ... doesn't trust the Labour Party at all. He goes on at length about how, after the war, the Labour Party gave all the work of building state houses to Fletchers instead of spreading it around amongst small contractors. He says they'll always back big business rather than risk losing votes.

"But Social Credit," he says, pouring more sherry into my glass before I have a chance to stop him, "they're for the little people. They'll give low-interest loans that'll give small businesses a chance to get ahead. That's what Kiwi life's all about, giving the little people a go. And what about what this Douglas bloke's planning?" he demands.

"Tuh, economics, I don't understand any of that," I reply. There's a cruel draught from the open door that I try to avoid by moving around so my back's against the wall. "That's not important anyway."

I take a mouthful of sherry and launch into an account of the inclusiveness Labour will bring to Muldoon's divided nation. I bring out all the catch-cries we have embraced in our search for a better way of life – nuclear-free, equal rights for women, gays and Maori, protection of the environment. It's dry work, arguing politics. I drink more sherry. He tops up my glass as soon as I put it down and I drink some more.

"All that's a sop to you loony Lefties," he sneers. "They'll sell out to big business. You see if they don't."

"But voting for Social Credit's just splitting the vote," I yell back banging the table with my fist and spilling sherry all over my hand. I lick it off before spitting out, "Do you want Muldoon to get back in again?"

Suddenly Old Tom's over my side of the table, hemming me in against the wall. He has his arms around me. His whiskery face scratches my cheek when I turn away from his kiss. My stomach lurches at his breath. It smells of alcohol, cigarettes and age. I'm appalled. I stagger up, oppressed by the fetid atmosphere. My chair tips over and clatters on the ground. I thrust him away – trying to get outside, out into the fresh air.

He backs off immediately, prolific with his apologies. "I'm a gentleman," he protests. "When a lady says 'no' that means 'no' but you can't blame a bloke for trying."

I'm squinting in the glare of the afternoon sun. I just want to get away but he insists we go out to the garden where vegetables stand in rows in black, well-tilled soil behind the garage. He fills a rice sack with broccoli, carrots, leeks, a good-sized cabbage and some late beans; enough to keep us in veges for days.

Almost worth being molested, sniggers Harshly Critical. With a frightening whoosh his fire bursts into flames.

I totter on down the road on legs that keep bending at odd angles, as if they've developed a mind of their own. When I'm out of sight of Old Tom's shack I huddle on the beach, down below the line of dinghies upturned on the grass verge, out of sight of the men messing about on their boats or yarning over on the wharf.

Well that went well, sneers Harshly Critical. I quail before the fury of his fire.

Still, quavers Blythe Spirit, *You've got all these nice veges.*

The shell-speckled beach gives way to sand smoothed by the out-going tide. Boats float seaward at their moorings. Over in Jacob's Bay the bus heads down the road from the school.

High Anxiety rises up in a panic. *Oh no,* she shrills. *You won't be home when the kids get back from school. They'll be so worried.*

Straight there, straight back it was meant to be, Stern Discipline roars from his great height. *At least you could show a bit of backbone if you're going to get drunk all the time. Come on now. Pull yourself together.*

But it has all become too much. I wrap my arms around my legs, rest my head against my knees and give way to a deluge of tears. The sack of vegetables lies forgotten beside me. And then, as if things weren't bad enough, footsteps are scrunching over the shells towards me.

Someone's coming. Hide! Hide! High Anxiety sinks completely into the muddy depths.

I hope I might be invisible, crouching there with my arms covering my head, but Paul's already seen me. He's so kind – sitting down next to me and waiting until I've gathered myself together.

"You've got some nice veges there," he says when I have taken some deep breaths and can raise my head.

I'm looking straight ahead. I don't yet have the wherewithal to face him but I'm relieved to find that I can answer calmly. "Yes aren't they? Old Tom gave them to me."

"Ah ... and shared some vile grog with you too, no doubt."

"Yes," I confess, "I am a little drunk and late too." My voice wobbles and I hollow out my throat to contain it. "The kids'll be getting home from school and wondering where I am."

"Kate'll be there though, won't she? She'll take care of them until you get back."

"Maybe ... but Janey'll be worried. It's just so hard for her to fit in at school. She didn't even want to go this morning." I gaze over at the point as if I could see through it to the boat-shed, to my children coming home and me not there. "I'm such a hopeless, hopeless mother." My lips are pressed hard against my teeth and my knees held tightly to my chest to hold in the tears.

Paul puts his arm around me. It's been so long since I last felt sheltered in a man's arms that I forget all about Lizzie and dissolve into him. I wonder if he will kiss me but he stands up and turns away to his dinghy.

"Don't be so hard on yourself," he says. "I should be heading back now anyway. I'll drop you off. You won't be that far behind them."

Ripples spreading out in our wake leave a rent through the glassy sea. Drips, falling from the oars as they lift out of the water, float away in a line of tiny circles. On a rock beyond the point a shag is holding out its wings to dry. I sit in the stern, my legs between Paul's stretched-out ones, watching the play of his muscles as he rows. I would like to reach out and touch him but I don't dare.

"How are you getting on with the book?" Paul asks as we round the point.

I want to say something deep and meaningful but I'm too drunk. I readjust the sack of vegetables on my lap to give me time to think.

"Great, really interesting ... although ... I mean ... how do they know all that stuff if they can't even see these particles? It all seems a bit nebulous to me."

He talks at length about bubble chambers, photographic tracks, computers and mathematical analysis as he rows me to shore but I'm really none the wiser.

"Mind-blowing stuff though, isn't it?" he ends as the dinghy scrapes the shingle.

"Sure is." I scramble out and give the dinghy a shove to launch it again.

"Thanks," I yell and trudge up to the boat ramp with my load of vegetables. When I turn back he's already pulling off around the point towards Jacob's Bay. He's looking back towards the wharf and doesn't even notice me when I wave.

He knows that you don't understand anything, Harshly Critical gloats.

I hurry up the path and burst into the boatshed calling out, "Hey kids, I'm home. Sorry I'm late but look at all the lovely veges I've got."

There's no reply. The books, toys, clothes and crayons are still scattered around. Dirty dishes and food scraps still cover the bench and table. The only change is the school bags flung on the floor.

They're not here. Oh no, where've they gone?

I sink on to a food bin and gaze around the shed in a blur of despair, nauseous with High Anxiety's agitation.

This is what happens when you get drunk with randy old men, rasps Harsh Criticism. His fire's burning so steadily now there's no need for extra stoking. I'm thoroughly submerged in the mire.

Stern Discipline takes control. *Pull yourself together. At least you've got a decent dinner to offer them tonight. If you are sober enough to cook it, that is,* he adds sourly.

I push through the flax and am met by Tracey scowling face. She's helping Thad build a hut in the puriri tree.

"Where have you been?" she shrills. "Janey's been wailing away like a total baby. What was I meant to do? I had to bring her up here to shut her up."

"Honey, I'm so sorry." I move over to stare pleadingly up at her. "Old Tom came by and suggested I go back with him to get some veges. I really didn't mean to be so long. But ... look ... I'm here now. No harm done, eh?"

Tracey turns her back on me. "Here, what about this bit?" she calls up to Thad.

You're putting way too much responsibility on her shoulders, growls Harshly Critical. *She's only seven, after all.*

Everything's all right though because Janey's now playing happily with Melissa. Flash Kate's in a good mood so I stay for a coffee, even though my soul feels burnt to a crisp, and tell her about my day without mentioning what happened with Old Tom. By the time I finally hurry the children back down the track the shadows have already overtaken the boatshed. High Anxiety's burrowing out my stomach, leaving a hollow that's difficult to ignore, but at least there's fish and fresh vegetables for dinner.

Boundaries

Grandfather Thaddeus was a small town banker, a prudent manager and canny investor. He died in the spring of '75, during Kate's last year at school, leaving his widow well-provided for and a small legacy of $5,000 to each of his grandchildren, Kate and her older brother, Guy, skipping a generation because he never had approved of his only child marrying a man of religion.

Unwisely maybe, not expecting to be cast down by a random heart attack quite so early in life – he was, after all only in his early 70s – he made no provision for the money to be tied up until the children reached a responsible age. Guy, being a chip off the old block, made knowledgeable investments. Kate blew the first thousand on a holiday to Bali during the University mid-year break the following year. She named Thad after his great-grandfather because without this legacy he would never have been conceived.

Naturally her parents were appalled, especially as Kate had nothing to say about the other essential contributor to this disaster. However her father maintained that Christian folks do not turn their backs on their children, no matter how much disgrace they have brought on the family. He searched about for a post far enough away that the shame would not follow them and, at the end of Kate's first and only year at University, they left the central North Island, where she had grown up, and moved to Howick.

Kate did her best to repay the heavy debt owed for this sacrifice by running the household and keeping the accounts in order. Her mother busied herself with the many social events the larger parish demanded and put it about that Kate's husband had died in tragic circumstances to explain why she was a housebound solo mother.

For four long years she carried this burden of guilt, until an old school friend tracked her down and rescued her, took her off for one fun Labour Weekend to the Island. Pete noticed her at the Surf Club, dancing in a world of her own, overwhelmed by the unaccustomed press of bodies around her. Having noticed her, he made his move and in the wee small hours she found herself stumbling up the Wairua track through looming shadows cast by a sated moon.

It took two more acrimonious weeks before she finally broke free from her parents' grasp, gathered up Thad and her barest essentials and returned to the island. Further disgrace was heaped on the family when another bastard child arrived the following November. Her mother's lips were seamed with martyred forbearance through all the days that Kate waited at their home for the birth. But grandchildren are grandchildren after all. Concessions have to be made if grandparents are to see anything of them.

Lately, however, her disgrace had been somewhat mitigated in her mother's eyes – the years of being a vicar's wife having not completely obliterated the banker's daughter. For Kate had used the last of her legacy to purchase a section on the island, had applied for a suspensory loan and was preparing to make a home for her and the children. Everyone knows that you can never go wrong with real estate.

Ah yes, the section, the house. At first it was what got Kate out of bed every morning at first light. Weeks went by, however, with nothing done. Now doubts held her in bed long after she heard the click-click of Lilith tiptoeing up the stairs and the whining at her bedroom door began.

She needed Pete's help but her house was his last concern, although he had not come out actively against it. It was just that other people had stronger claims on him that took him off for weeks at a time and when he got back he spent all his time up at Wairua.

Then there were the plans that had to be drawn up before she could apply for a building permit. She had unburdened herself to Angel at her Gemini party and Angel was quick to offer Eddie's help. She said he could build it too if Pete was too busy and brought him by the next morning to discuss it. They stayed well into the afternoon and Eddie drew some sketches of what she wanted – between coffees and gossip about the party, of course. But nothing had eventuated out of this initial enthusiasm.

She applied for the suspensory loan for first-home buyers, sent the forms away weeks ago. It was for $5000, which was written off if the owner lived in the house for seven years. But there was still no response from there either.

Lying in bed, enjoying her first cigarette of the day, she pondered the tarot reading Lou had done for her the previous week when they returned from Play Centre. It was a lack-lustre reading with only three Major Arcana – *The Empress* crowning her, *The Hierophant* behind her, and *The Lovers* reversed as her hopes and fears – meaning failure and foolish designs. The culminating card was the ten of pentacles, which suggested eventual success. Lou had advised patience. Kate wondered what a stranger would make of the cards. She suspected Lou of interpreting the cards according to her own view of how Kate's life should run.

At least sunlight was filtering in from the windows behind her so it might be a fine day and Melissa could play out on the deck. She rolled over and squinted up at the moon calendar dangling from the rafters. The moon was moving into Libra this morning, promising a harmonious day. Perhaps, if Mouse was not too hung-over, she would have her up for a game of Scrabble once the chores were done.

Flash Kate had taken a long time to warm to Mouse. It had annoyed her that Lou brought Mouse around to look at the boat-shed without asking first. Grudgingly she had taken them down to peer through the window of the boat-shed and had given them the number to call, hoping all the while that Mouse would find something more suitable and they could continue to have the beach to themselves.

It was awkward at first. Mouse hid whenever they went down there but Kate could feel her presence pulsating behind the corrugated-iron walls. However after a while it became so normal it was like nothing had changed, except that the children now had friends to play with. Tracey was enough of a tomboy to keep up with Thad and Janey was always happy to entertain Melissa.

Only when the weather closed in did she start to wonder about Mouse. Pete sailed away the day after her birthday, not even waiting for the weekend and the Gemini party she had spent so much time planning. He said he had to go when the weather was right. That he took Patsy with him only added to the insult.

Her feelings were in such an uproar that she went down to the boat-shed on the pretext of inviting Mouse to her party, and had her up to play Scrabble as a distraction from the circularity of her thoughts. Mouse turned out to be good company: a good listener and a challenging Scrabble player. She could be funny too if the song was anything to go by. It was a shame about the song but Kate doubted any of the others would really want to put on a performance, not when it came down to it.

Lilith gave a tentative scratch at the bedroom door. There had been movement downstairs for a while but now the children's voices were raised.

"Melissa!" Thad was yelling. "Don't you touch it. You mess up my fort you'll be sorry."

Thad had ignored her repeated demands to clear away his toys before bed last night, even though she tried to be strict about this. The sea-grass mat in front of the ranch sliders was covered with every one of his blocks and whatever else he could find to build a towering fort.

"I don't have to do what you say. I only have to do what Mummy says." As usual, Melissa was defiant in the face of a larger force.

"I'm warning you." Thad's voice vibrated with menace.

Lilith's scratches became more insistent.

A crash of tumbling bricks … the sounds of flesh impacting on flesh … Melissa wailing.

Kate was out of bed in an instant and glaring down at Thad from the balcony. Lilith scuttled down the stairs, her tail tucked out of sight.

He stared up at her. His fists were clenched at his sides. The scattered blocks lay all around him.

"Did you hit her?" she yelled.

"I told her not to go near my fort. Look what she's done. It's all wrecked now." Thad was trembling with fury.

Kate bounded down the stairs. She stood over him.

He stepped back out of her reach without taking his eyes from her face.

"I told you to get that cleared up last night, didn't I? But no, you had to leave it. Now look what's happened. You do not hit your sister, understand?" She raised her hand.

He turned his back on her and began firing the blocks into their basket.

Melissa huddled into a corner of the leather sofa, crying softly and clutching Foxy to her.

"You realize that's a dead animal," Kate shouted at her.

But Melissa only tightened her grip on Foxy and stifled her tears by putting her thumb in her mouth.

Kate knew she should leave it at that but a rant swelled up from her frustrated loins and continued to spill out all the while she was dressing, feeding the dog, starting the fire, cooking the breakfast and making Thad's school lunch. Thad tuned her out and got ready for school as if he were alone in the house. Melissa refused to move off the sofa, even when she was called for breakfast, so that Kate had to pick her up and carry her to the table.

With the rant having exhausted itself they ate in silence. As soon as he heard the bus passing on its way down to the wharf, Thad left without saying goodbye. Kate lingered at the table, drinking coffee and smoking, until she heard it pull away, making its way back over the hill to Jacob's Bay. Melissa was huddled back on the sofa, a little bundle of misery wrapped around a fur stole.

It took until mid-morning for Kate to work off her rage. She was filling the empty spaces of the day by helping Melissa cut some shapes out of biscuit dough when Mouse crossed the deck and poked her head in at the ranch sliders.

"I'm making some stock with the fish frame," she announced. "Do you mind if I grab a few herbs?"

"Of course, help yourself," Kate answered. "We're doing some baking. You can come in for a coffee if you want."

It irritated Kate that Mouse could never just accept her overtures. She always had to go over them in her mind first, as if she was searching for some ulterior motive. And when she eventually did deign to toe off her boots and come into the house, she always edged herself into the chair nearest the sloping ceiling so that she had to lean forward over the table, instead of sitting further out in the room,

"How's your head this morning?" Kate asked her.

"Good."

"I'm making bears and stars," Melissa told her. She turned to look at Mouse from her perch on a chair at the breakfast bar.

"Good," Mouse said again.

She seemed even more fidgety than usual this morning: sitting up straight in her chair with her hands in her pockets and her chin on her chest, then subsided on to her elbows again, back and forth.

"So what are you up to this morning?" Kate asked her once the biscuits were in the oven.

"Housework," said Mouse. She straightened up again, laid her hands flat on the table and, on the outward surge of a deep breath, announced,

"I've got the verses."

"Verses?" Kate shook the kettle to feel its level and moved over to the sink to fill it.

"Melissa you go through to the bathroom and wash your hands now, sweetie. You can have a tea-party with your dolls out on the deck when the biscuits are cooked."

"And Foxy too!" trilled Melissa. She scrambled down from the chair and caught up Foxy from the sofa. Her mother's lips thinned.

Mouse's mouth was resting on her fists. She stared down at the space between her elbows.

"Verses," said Kate. "Now don't get me wrong, it's a great song ... really. Just don't be disappointed if the others find an excuse to back out. Believe me, I've seen it before ... full of enthusiasm until they need to do something ... then nothing. "

Mouse shielded her eyes with her hands and continued to stare at the table top. In a vacuum so expansive that every sound seemed to bounce right back at her, Kate cleaned up after the baking and helped Melissa set up her little table and chairs out on the deck with her various dolls and stuffed toys gathered around. Once the coffee had been made, and a plastic teapot of lemon drink for Melissa, Kate tried to fill the vacuum with an account of her problems with her section. But even when she put Mouse's coffee down in front of her and offered her a biscuit Mouse remained off somewhere else entirely.

"Oh, all right then, tell me," Kate snapped. She took out the makings of a cigarette and started to roll it.

"Doesn't matter. You're probably right," muttered Mouse. "I'm just being stupid. I should go."

"No, go on, just tell me."

Mouse eyed her from beneath the cage of her arms. "You really want to hear it?" she asked.

Kate sighed. She lit her cigarette.

"There'll be no peace until you have it out of your system so you might as well get it over with," she drawled through a cloud of smoke.

Words stumbled over one another as Mouse, straightened up against the sloping roof, hands flying here and there, outlined how the floorshow would go, stopping to sing the verses in the appropriate places. When she had finished she looked over at Kate.

Kate drew on her cigarette. "It's not bad," she conceded. "It would certainly rattle a few cages."

"See the others would just have to stand at the bar and be themselves, just sing the choruses," Mouse pleaded. "You could play the part of the other woman," she added.

"And the man?"

Mouse's hands were clasped as if she were in prayer, her knuckles white with tension. "I thought, maybe, Paul would do it," she murmured.

"Paul? I don't think that's a very good idea," said Kate, well aware of the suspicions Lizzie had been sharing around. Instead her mind roved over certain considerations to do with Patsy and Pete and ideas of freedom.

"Richie seems keen," she mused. "We could ask him." She stubbed out her cigarette in the paua shell beside her. "I suppose there's no harm in seeing what the others think."

Satisfied with this vote of confidence Mouse settled down to listen to Kate's problems.

"Isn't there anything you can do?" she asked when the monologue had petered out. "Maybe I could help."

Melissa came running in with her teapot, wanting more lemon drink because her dolls had drunk all of it and there was none for her and Foxy. Kate refused to make more lemon drink and said that she would just have to drink water, which sent Melissa into a tantrum. Finally Kate relented, fetched another lemon from the garden, mixed her up more drink and carried it out to the deck.

"Now you make sure you drink all that yourself this time," she ordered.

When she returned to the table she began rolling another cigarette but Mouse had already finished her coffee and was getting up to leave.

"I do need to find the boundary pegs," Kate said to stall her departure. "I know where one is but I need to find the others. Pete left me a long tape measure and a compass but it really needs two people. I need a machete too, to clear away the undergrowth."

"I've got a machete," Mouse put in eagerly. "You know, I told you last night. Old Tom lent me one to clear away that green-weed for a garden. We could do it this afternoon. It's such a nice day it would be good to be out in it."

"We could, but what about Melissa? She has to have an afternoon nap or she falls asleep at five and then wants to stay up all night."

Out on the deck Melissa was feeding a small cup of lemon drink to Foxy. The fur was sticky with drink.

"I could ask Patsy to mind her, I suppose. And I could ring the school and tell them the children are to go there when they get out. Do you want to stay for an early lunch and then we'll go? I wouldn't think it would take more than an hour," she enthused. "After all, how hard can it be?"

Well, quite hard as it turned out. By the time Kate and Mouse returned, all tattered and torn from slashing through thick undergrowth to find Patsy, Lou and Richie ensconced in the kitchen. The older children had already had their afternoon tea and had dispersed in all directions, . And, despite Kate's anxieties, Melissa, who was playing in the yard with Gabe, was not pleased to see her.

"Go away, Mummy," she cried. "I'm playing with Gabe."

A rueful laugh spilled from Kate. "That's okay, honey. We're going to stop for a while anyway."

Brandishing a bottle of Stone's green ginger wine she had felt compelled to buy for Patsy to make amends, Kate threw open the kitchen door and flopped down at the table. Mouse slipped in behind her, confident enough now to sit down without waiting to be invited.

"Phew, I'm exhausted," Kate exclaimed. "Sorry we're so late. It took longer than I thought but at last it's done. My territory has been defined. I think that calls for a drink! I hope Melissa wasn't any trouble."

"Not at all," replied Patsy. She got up from her armchair, displacing the cat from her lap, and got out the glasses. "She helped me beat Richie at Euchre and then Lou arrived with Gabe and they've been playing happily ever since."

Richie was sprawled in the other armchair. He had been picking out tunes on Patsy's guitar, trying to find a song that they all knew the words to, and now fell into exploring the permutations of the last riff he had been playing. The cat settled down by his feet. His front paws were tucked primly beneath him and one ear was twitched back.

"And you're back again, Lou," went on Kate. "Not a lot of joy at the spiritual home?"

Lou had been surveying the cards, still scattered across the table amongst the remains of afternoon tea, with a jaundiced eye and finally gave in to the urge to clear the table.

"I just came down to collect the boys," she told Kate as she moved from table to bench and back again. "But since you ask, no, they're not. If I have to listen to Joe going on about Atlantis and the likelihood of spacemen being on Earth once more I think I'll go mad. Honestly, who cares? He's obviously been spending too much time alone because he's become obsessed ... wants to set up a telescope upstairs so he can watch for UFOs."

"I saw a UFO once, out in the desert," said Richie. "I was camping out there with some other guys. This circle of flashing lights skimmed across the sky. We all saw it. Of course no one believed us. The government, you know, they keep a lid on all that."

Lou dismissed him with a glare and turned back to Kate. "It's obviously just another excuse to turf us out of the attic. And he does nothing to help. Just lies around all day reading these books and raving about it every mealtime. And Horse Fly's suddenly taken up eating with us again. At least he chops some firewood occasionally but neither of them contributes any cash. Joe spent all Tuesday working over at the Lodge and do you think he shared any of the money? Nothing. Just because I'm on the DPB they think they can bludge off me all the time."

Her gaze settled on a point somewhere above the settee. "I've a good mind to go back to Wellsford and stay with the old man for a while."

The words flickered through the room like a slight breeze presaging the first storm of autumn. The other ladies stared at her. Richie fingered a slow arpeggio.

"Wellsford? But you don't even get on with your old man," protested Patsy. She was ensconced in her armchair again, leaving Kate to pour the wine, and now squirmed around to glare at Lou, who was leaning against the bench.

"Well where else can I go?" cried Lou. "The dream's over. I'm sick to death of this island, of Wairua and everything. Who knows, I might even be able to get a job there at the maternity hospital."

Patsy leapt up to stoke the fire with much clamour. She moved a simmering pot of beans to the back of the stove. Outside Melissa shrieked with laughter. The wine glugged into the glasses and Kate handed them around. Richie laid the guitar aside and stretched his legs out, shoving the cat out of position so that it got up and stalked, tail lashing, to the door.

"It's just a thought," Lou reassured Patsy. She used the pretext of letting the cat out to keep her back to them and her emotions concealed. "I won't make any definite decision until after the ball."

"Speaking of the ball," gushed Flash Kate, anxious to move the conversation on to something more congenial. "Mouse has come up with some verses and a floorshow. I think it will be quite good. I'm going to play the other woman. Tell them about it Mouse."

There was silence when Mouse finished telling them her idea.

Patsy was the first to speak. "So what would we have to do?" she asked doubtfully.

"Well, you just have to stand at the bar and sing the choruses," explained Mouse. "Maybe you could swing your mugs back and forth in time to the music and then we'll all link arms and do the dance at the end. You just have to be you, really"

"If I can even remember the words," muttered Patsy.

"Well we'll all be singing it so it won't matter if you don't know them all." Mouse's finger smeared through a circle of wine her glass had left on the table top.

"Who's going to play the man?" Lou asked, getting up to get the dishcloth to wipe it up.

Mouse gave a veiled look over at Richie, who had picked up the guitar again and was working through a riff.

"We thought you might do it, Richie," Kate said.

The question hung in the air until the women's eyes upon him roused him from his reverie.

"Ah, sorry, were you talking to me?" he asked.

"We thought you might be in the floorshow. You know, Mouse's song. We need a man," Kate told him.

"Oh." He strummed through a chord change. A faint smile twitched his lips. "Yeah, why not? What do I have to do?"

Patsy barely allowed Mouse to finish her explanation before she began to object. "Why does she get to be the other woman? If anyone's going to cuddle up to Richie it should be me."

"It's only acting, babe," said Richie. "It doesn't mean anything."

"And I've acted before," Kate answered. "We always put on a show at the end of the year when I did dancing lessons so I'm used to being on stage." She stared steadily through Patsy's scowl. "Anyway a moment ago you were wondering if you would even remember the words to the song so how would you manage anything more?"

"We'll have to see what Lizzie thinks, anyway," said Lou. "Let's try it out on Saturday. I'd better get my boys rounded up now though or we won't get up the track before dark."

Work On What Has Been Spoiled

Out of a glorious sleep I surface into a body that's so clean. Even the sheets feel fresh and crisp against my skin.

Dinner and hot baths at Kate's last night, it doesn't get much better than this, cries Blythe Spirit. *And it's mail day today.*

Harshly Critical allows me little time for bliss, however, before he starts his morning demolition. *You've been out all week, gallivanting around, spending money like it's going out of fashion. You're making such a fool of yourself. They're all laughing at you.*

High Anxiety whimpers as Stern Discipline calls down the inventory for the day. *Tidy up, do dishes, sheets and towels washed, cook rice, make bread ... the bread that's left is so stale that the girls will have to buy pies for lunch ... not that you can afford it ... and you still haven't picked up any seaweed off the beach. All those fine days, gone to waste. No mail day for you today.*

Yeah. It's not like you ever get any mail anyway, puts in Harshly Critical.

I turn away to the window. Out in the bay, beyond the naked sand, a pathway of sunlight reflects off the crinkled water.

Tracey pokes her head above the ladder. "Mum, you getting up? It's way after seven."

"So much good stuff to eat this week," declares Tracey. She tips her porridge bowl up to drink the last of the milk. "Pork chops on Sunday, mince on Tuesday, fish on Wednesday, dinner with Kate and them last night and we even get to buy a pie for lunch today. It's choice!"

"We're all nice and clean too," adds Janey.

"Things certainly do seem to be looking up," I reply. "You're even enjoying school more, Janey."

"That's 'cause she's got a boyfriend," sneers Tracey. "He showed her his eel," she smirks.

"Nick's got a pet eel up the creek from Patsy's." Janey's happier than I've seen her in ages. "We took it some bread yesterday. He's sad though 'cause he's got to go back to Wairua and there'll be no one to feed it."

"Nick and Janey up a tree ..." Tracey starts chanting.

"He's not ... he's not ... he's not my boyfriend," cries Janey and throws herself on Tracey trying to hit her.

But Tracey fends her off laughing, "Yes he is. Yes he is."

"Cut it out Tracey," I say. "Come on, get your bags together. The bus went over to the wharf a few minutes ago. You'll miss it if you don't hurry."

Once they've left I dredge one last cuppa out of the teapot and sit drinking it in the deserted boatshed. The bus drones up the road from the wharf and comes to a stop. Then it starts up again and carries on back to Jacob's Bay. There are heaps of muddy clothes, an amorphous jumble in the gloom beneath the loft. Tracey's duvet dangles off the top bunk. Janey has left her soft toys spread around the back of the boatshed where a heavy bedspread breathes against the draught coming through the double doors that open on to the boat ramp.

Nothing to look forward to but housework, moans Harshly Critical. His fire is burning with a steady glow. *Most women have time for other things because they keep on top of it but not you, oh no. You let the likes of that Flash Kate suck up your time instead. Not that you'll get any thanks for it, mind.*

At least I'd stacked the dishes and changed the sheets before I went up to Kate's yesterday but there's a putrid smell mingling with the usual dampness that's impossible to ignore. It takes me a while to discover the snapper frame that I was going to make it into stock. I only meant to grab some herbs and tell Flash Kate about the verses but the delight of sitting in her warm house overcame Stern Discipline's scruples and now a whole day's been lost. The fish frame's no good for soup now. I throw it in the piss bucket so I can empty it in the compost when I go up for my morning shit.

The fire's lit and I've packed up the breakfast dishes so it's time for a coffee and joint out here on my beer-crate. Sunlight struggles to make any headway against the chill but at least it's warmer than inside the boatshed.

Blythe Spirit whirls around and around on her pinnacle, very excited about the reception my verses received. I can't believe it really might happen and the only way I can keep High Anxiety in check is by not thinking about it at all. Nevertheless I feel like I'm floating on an updraft. We're having our first rehearsal on Saturday afternoon.

Tomorrow, in fact, screams High Anxiety.

I hug myself to contain her panic and focus on a pleasing harmony of kanuka trunks that are catching the sun up on the point.

Those sheets need to go out on the line if they're to dry before nightfall, says Stern Discipline to bring me back to the job in hand.

I pound the sheets up and down in the tub. My shoulder muscles are stiff from all that slashing yesterday and a blister under the callus below my right little finger is stinging.

Offering to help that bitch was a big mistake. You spent hours hacking through the undergrowth, Harshly Critical moans.

But it seemed only right, seeing as she had been good enough to listen to me tell about the verses.

Yesterday, while we were slashing through a mess of ferns, flaxes and shrubby mingi mingi, Kate told me how they used to move every few years when she was a kid. That's just what vicars do evidently.

She'd just get to feel at home and they'd be off again. She wants what we all want: a secure home for her kids to grow up in, a proper garden with fruit trees, a lemon tree, and a grapevine growing over the verandah, a place to belong.

"All I ever wanted was to be part of the stories everyone told," she confided as we laid the tape over the area we had just cleared and she set the compass again to check we were still heading in the right direction. "I thought Wairua was it, but they already had their stories and, once again, I wasn't part of them. I need a place of my own to make my own stories."

I suggested to her that just by making this start, other things would happen. It's like untangling a knot. Once you've found an end the rest comes apart quite easily. And I reminded her of how I needed to move out of the Bay long before I did but things only started to happen when Big Lou told me about the boat-shed.

"She brought me down talk to you about it and the next thing Pete was picking up my stuff in his boat and we were moved in. It was a blessing from God, all of it, how it happened."

Flash Kate rolled her eyes at this – for a vicar's daughter she sure has a low opinion of God – but then we were distracted by a tangle of supple-jack and the conversation waned.

I'm hanging the sheets on the line when Harshly Critical blows on his embers and reminds me of the really stupid gaffe I made yesterday when the kids had been rounded up and we were preparing to leave. My face drenches hot with shame. And yet, how was I to know? I was just saying that Gabe looks more like Lou, not tall, stringy and fair like the boys' father. However, later, when Kate and I were discussing it over some of her marigold wine after dinner, she smiled knowingly and said that there was more to it than that.

It seems that Gabe was conceived around the night of their Harvest Festival – which is a celebration they have every year on the weekend closest to the autumn equinox. Angel was new to the island then and all the men were hanging around her, especially Tom. This really bummed Lou out because Nick was still on the tit and sucking her dry so she was feeling all ugly and cow-like: particularly vulnerable. Well, Kate said, that later that evening Big Lou went off somewhere with Aussie Joe. They were away for hours.

Kate said that everyone knows this because Nick had woken up and wailed most of the time she'd been away. Tom made a big scene when they got back because trying to calm Nick had cramped his style no end with Angel. That's the real reason, Flash Kate said, that he left. He thinks Gabe is Aussie Joe's kid. And so does Aussie Joe, which is why Lou and Aussie Joe don't get on. It's because she won't even admit the possibility.

Harshly Critical snorts derisively. *And you thought it was because Lou liked you that she's always so sympathetic about Angel.*

Pain wells up. I peg the last sheet on the line and return to the shed to start the bread and the dishes.

Stern Discipline whispers in time with my steps, *Get a grip ... get a grip ... get a grip.*

But then Blythe Spirit reminds me that Flash Kate wouldn't have shared this secret with me if she didn't consider me a confidante to be trusted.

She likes you. All that work you did for her yesterday: finding the boundary pegs, chopping all that firewood, even sharing some of Old Tom's veges; you earned that dinner and those baths. Yes! Life's wonderful and only going to get better!

I've followed the sun up on to the bank by the fire pit and am basking in the satisfaction of a job well done. Order has been restored to the boat-shed. The sheets flap in the rising wind and the previous day's washing is laid out in the loft, airing in the afternoon sun. I've enjoyed a crusty slice of warm bread slathered in butter, Vegemite, garlic and parsley and now there's coffee and a joint to follow. My boots and socks lie beside me. The sun toasts my pale winter shins. Wavelets break gently on the shingle and suck it seaward while a lone seagull cries as it wheels off over towards the wharf.

I dream of Fissure Bay: that gash between hills that's like a womb scooped out between the ridges. In the summer time I walked naked all day, surrounded by the rustling sounds of bush and water, feeling like I was part of a living being. There's a pool in the creek surrounded by black rock where I would lie, heating up in the sun before plunging into the cool water that's so soft it feels like swimming in silk. The bay itself falls away just as steeply as the land. Schools of little blue mau mau flit by in the clear depths, octopuses conceal themselves in dark holes amongst the kelp and fat paua, only visible to a discerning eye, blend with the pink-covered rocks. A longing to be there eats away at my soul.

Stern Discipline nudges me out of my reverie. *That was then, this is now,* he rasps. *Where are you going to put this garden?*

The area beyond the boat-shed would make a good-sized garden only it's shaded for most of the day at this time of year. Old Tom's lent me the machete to clear the green-weed but I don't know if that's really where I want a garden. I guess it'll be good in summer.

Yeah, when you have to move out because the owners are coming back for the holidays, grouses Harshly Critical. *And it'll take forever to dig out the roots of that green-weed.*

I could dig out the kikuyu spilling down the slope from the long-drop but it doesn't seem a very healthy spot to grow vegetables. You can tell the consistency of your morning shit by the sound of the splash it makes.

Paul is pulling his way back to Jacob's Bay but he's looking over to the wharf and doesn't notice my wave. How good it must be to have strong muscles like a man and to understand physics like he can.

Yesterday morning I read about emptiness and form. Within the emptiness ... but can one even say 'within'? Emptiness is the field on which all potential form exists. But even 'field' suggests enclosure so that's not right. It's hard to envisage limitless space when we are defined by boundaries. Anyway ... there's the Void.

Maybe it's like the boat-shed, which provides an empty space for us to live out our lives. If time were sped up you could see the dance, the changing foci of energies. In the beginning everything is in its appointed place but time passes and things change in relation to each other. If the weather is wet there are piles of muddy clothes and a scatter of toys. If it's fine, things return to order. Raw produce joins in a relation with heat to form food, which breaks down to grow bodies. And time too plays its part. Months ago Flash Kate signed the deeds to her section so the fish frame rotted in its pot.

And yet that's not it at all because it doesn't convey the interactions of energy that create change. An electron emits a photon, which is energy, and it is absorbed by another electron causing both to veer away from each other. There is no force, only an interaction.

But at this point my brain turns to mush and I arrive back at the only thing that I took from this chapter, which is that the Void holds the potentiality of all that exists. Everything is a part of the whole so that even the smallest particles exist as they relate to the whole, which is the Void.

A part ... nothing is apart. How funny it is that 'a part' – two separate words – relates to the whole, whereas 'apart' – with no gap – denies the whole.

Come on; make a decision, snaps the part of me that is Stern Discipline.

The lines of the *I Ching* are firm or yielding but their significance depends on the relationship they have with one another. Sometimes it's best to hold firm, at others it's better to be yielding. It all depends on what's appropriate to the time.

Neither is light or shade inherently good in itself ... like now, choosing a space for a garden. A garden needs as much sun as it can get in the winter but in the summer a little shade helps to retain moisture.

And large is not necessarily better than small. What is the point of breaking in a large garden if I don't end up staying? And why plan a summer garden if I'm not going to be here to tend it over the driest months? A smaller garden that'd keep us in fresh greens is all we really need.

I stand up and gaze around me. Maybe right here, where I've been sitting, is the best place. It gets most of the afternoon sun and the long-drop drains the other way. I could use that good-sized pohutukawa bough that washed up in the storm last week. It would hold up a sizable bed if I cut into the slope just here, along a bit from the fire so I still have a place to sit to enjoy my lunch.

The half-smoked joint dangles from my fingers.

Blythe Spirit swirls around her boa with a lazy motion. *May as well finish the joint first,* she whispers.

I sit down again and search around for the matches.

You need to get started, commands Stern Discipline, glaring down at me from his great height.

Their battle strobes against the warmth of the afternoon but eventually I pull on my socks and gumboots. Blythe Spirit's hollowing out the back of my throat with disappointment but I stash the remainder of the joint in the matchbox and go down to the beach to drag up the bough.

There's something so satisfying about the rhythm of physical labour. Yesterday's soreness wears off as I steadily dig soil out of the hillside to fill up the space framed by the bough. The garden I will plant arranges itself in my mind while I work. Mostly I like to grow edible greens – weeds, I call them – things like parsley, land cress, New Zealand spinach, rocket, borage and such: plants that are either perennial or self-seed so prolifically that, once established, they pop up all over the place. Such weeds certainly bulked up an otherwise bland diet in Fissure Bay. When the bed's ready we'll go in there for a visit and bring back some plants.

By the time the bus stops up on the road, I'm finishing the well-deserved joint while I contemplate my garden: one stride wide and three strides long. I'll bring up some seaweed from the beach once the girls have had their afternoon tea.

The girls work their way through a mug of Milo and a pile of bread and Vegemite while they tell me about their day.

Tracey's in a grump because Thad's gone to meet Kate at Patsy's again and she has no one to play with.

"We were going to work on our hut," she complains. "I guess I'll just have to play with old Boo Hoo here instead," she adds with a glance at Janey.

"Maybe Janey doesn't want to play with you," I snap. "I don't know why she would. You haven't been that nice to her lately."

But Janey's pathetically eager. "We could play Omma Lommas in the pohutukawa tree," she cries, her little voice vibrating with hope.

Tracey curls up her lip.

"You could always help me pick up seaweed instead," I suggest.

"Oh please," Janey pleads. "We haven't played Omma Lommas for ages."

Omma Lommas are a whole community of imaginary creatures that live in the bush. In Fissure Bay they kept the girls occupied for days at a time.

Tracey can't contain a snort of laughter. "Okay, but just this once. It's a bit babyish," she grins.

The bank of seaweed across the bay has been thrashing around in the surf for days now. It's all broken up and mixed with bush litter. The sweep of the waves has washed the bulk of it over by the rocks on the wharf side so I start there, scooping it into rice sacks.

A forget-me-not blue sky stretches out to the horizon without the faintest wisp of cloud. It's so warm that I'm still stripped down to my T-shirt. My toes wriggle freely in the cool shingle. The girls' laughter, as light as thistledown, floats across from the pohutukawa.

I fill four bags. Three of them cover my freshly dug soil and one goes on top of the compost heap. The girls are still playing happily so I take another two bags up to mulch the silver beet and the parsley.

But now the evening chill's settling and the sun's sinking into a bank of orange and pink so I call the girls and show them the finished bed.

"We'll go into Fissure Bay the next fine weekend after the ball and get some plants," I tell them.

"Yay, Fissure Bay," they crow, hugging one another and dancing around.

"I've been missing Fissure Bay so much," Tracey murmurs.

The door shuts out the cold night air and traps in the heat from the gas cooker. I stir-fry some rice, with onions, garlic, leeks, carrots, broad beans and parsley. At least there are more vegetables than rice this time. Janey's reading today's reader to Tracey. Their russet heads gleam in the patch of light that the candles hollow out of the darkness pressing around them.

I should change my t-shirt. It's wet from carrying the bags of seaweed and my back's all chilly despite my Swanni but I need to get the girls fed and it'll soon be time for bed anyway.

Over dinner Tracey asks me if they'll be going to the ball.

"Oh please, please," she begs. "The others are always getting to go out and we never do."

High Anxiety quivers inside me. The girls have both stopped eating and are watching me anxiously. Janey sucks at her fork but Tracey has laid hers down and is preparing for battle. I swallow a mouthful and shake my head.

"Not this time, honey. Lizzie wants it to be for adults only so none of the children will be going. You're going to have your own fun time at Patsy's though. She's going to find a babysitter for you, one of the teenagers probably. You're all going to stay at her place for the night – Thad and Melissa, and Lou's boys and Sam. You'll have a great time. "

"But we won't get to see the song," cries Tracey in dismay.

Janey has laid her fork down and they are both glaring at me. I scoop up the last grains of rice and chew thoughtfully.

"Well you'll definitely get to watch the dress rehearsal," I suggest, "and I need you to help me practice it. You can join in with the chorus while I sing the verses."

They help me clear away the dinner dishes and we sing the song through together, over and over. Then I fill the hot-water bottles while they clean their teeth and we all snuggle up together on Janey's bunk for their bedtime stories.

First Steps

The Beast Machine swooped around corners and up and down hills, bearing Big Lou and her boys away from her one-time haven, which now weighed on her like a life-long sentence. The older boys' energy had exacerbated the tension between her and Aussie Joe until, that morning, it burst out in a barrage of recrimination just because Ben and Nick, who were early risers, had disturbed Joe's last hours of sleep. Flinging back his coverings, with his tackle hanging free and his hair sticking out from his head every which way, he had raged at them until Lou hurtled down the steps from the attic to shout in return. Breakfast had been consumed amidst two escalating torrents of abuse that slapped against each other, rearing up and subsiding into a fragile lull before surging forth once more. The boys had gobbled down their porridge and disappeared outside, despite the blustery wind bending the trees in a savage dance. In the end there was nothing left to do but to flee once again down the winding road to Patsy's place, too early to decently arrive on someone's doorstep on a Saturday morning.

By Wednesday morning a stultifying permanency had settled on her, like the fog pressing against the windows and darkening the attic, leaving Monday's golden times as a fading dream lingering on the fringes of her mind. She had woken up squashed beneath the slope of the roof because Gabe, who had become accustomed to sharing a double bed with her at Patsy's place, had snuggled on to her single mattress during the night and was lying diagonally across it. The guilt of leaving Patsy's the day before without even waiting to catch up with Ben and Nick mingled with the mortification that had driven her away. For, from the time Richie had come in at the end of their shared lunch, he had never even glanced in her direction. Of course she had not expected anything else – not really – but, nevertheless, disappointment gnawed at her spirits. Saturday night's passion had changed nothing and neither had the three weeks away. The older boys' mattresses were piled with bags that needed unpacking but then what? Only long, lonely days.

All that day and Thursday morning had been taken up with unpacking and reconnecting with the kitchen and garden. With no rush to work to the school timetable she and Gabe had lingered in bed until she tired of reading *Harry the Dirty Dog* over and over and answering the 'when are Ben and Nick coming home' question yet again. But even with this late start the days still dragged.

Thursday afternoon saw her heading down to civilisation again, ostensibly to gather her boys up and bring them home, but really because there was nothing else she cared to do. Against the rattle of the car over the gravel road the refrain that had been humming in her head for weeks now played over and over – *'If not here, where?'*

Over lunch Aussie Joe's perpetual gloom had lightened a bit. He had been doing some work up at the Lodge the previous day and the manager, Rodney, had given him a telescope which he had bought second-hand. He wanted to use it to check on his boat if he didn't have time to get down to the wharf. But unfortunately it was an astronomical telescope and of no use to him. Also, the anarchist, Joe, had found that he had something in common with the capitalist, Rodney.

"He agrees that everything's bein' stymied by too much regulation,"

Joe told Big Lou through a mouthful of sandwich. "Everything'd run better if the government just kept out of it and left people free to do their own thing."

"Really?" Lou poured the tea and handed him a cup.

Gabe gulped down his Milo – *glunk, glunk, glunk* – and thumped his mug down on the table.

The hot water grumbled.

Joe swallowed the last of his sandwich and reached for more bread. "I reckon he's got a point," he went on. "Look at what's happenin' in this country. The government pays people to sit on their butts and do nothin' but stifles any kind of initiative. All those import and foreign currency restrictions, wage and price freezes: none of it's workin'. If people were freed up to serve their own interests things'd work much better."

Lying on her mattress later, with Gabe sleeping beside her, Lou had pondered where her interest lay. Her days were spent taking care of her boys, and she supposed it could be said that was serving her own interest, but who would care for them if she didn't? Their father had certainly taken care of his interests and was gone with the tide.

A kaka whistled in the puriri tree outside and then flew down the valley with a loud screech. The trees whispered with a passing breeze that sifted through the open window at the end of the attic and caused a cobweb she had missed in the rafters to sway in the updraft. And all the time the distant chatter of the creek.

Her few personal things were arranged on a tea chest next to her mattress: her tarot pack and book, hairbrush and comb, moisturiser, hand cream, the amethyst that Patsy had brought her back from town to aid her healing, and a small picture of her mother in a battered frame that she had carried with her since she first left the farm. She took up the cards and swirled them around, bringing the question for the first time out into the light of day: *If not here, where?*

Death was there again – before her so the transformation was still to come. Three fives indicated instability. *Strength* beneath her, brought out a grimace because strong was the last thing she was feeling. She worked through the cards one by one, reading their meanings and observing the feelings they invoked. The culminating card was the *6 of cups*, a card of childhood and memories.

Gabe stirred. She stroked a dark lock of hair off his forehead and got up to whisk the cobweb down with the Tarot book. Once she had fed and watered him they would go down and get the boys. That was what was needed. Their wild energy would soon perk up her spirits.

What would she do if she could just please herself? On Friday she played with the possibilities. She needed a place of her own where she could do things her way, with a private room where she could be alone with her stuff. If she had some land of her own, she could get a subsidy to build herself a home, just like Kate. But every cent of the benefit was taken up with keeping the boys fed. Maybe she could get a job when Gabe started school in another eighteen months, although they would have to start all over again somewhere else if she wanted to go nursing because the district nurse here showed no sign of wanting to move on.

Childhood memories. The words that had spilled out the afternoon before at Patsy's place were out of her mouth before she even realised what she was saying. They left her haunted by visions of the farm where she grew up – the light green of the willow trees down by the creek, the darker patch of native that sprouted out of the gully, the cow-spotted hills. She knew it wouldn't work.

Shortly after Lou had left to go nursing the old man had married Irene, the widow from the neighbouring farm, but Lou had long since made peace with her. Irene always made them welcome and never forgot to send the boys money on their birthdays. It was political differences with her father that kept her away. The Springbok Tour in 1981 had fractured their relationship forever. That year, even though it was close to Christmas, she had stayed with Belle in Ponsonby for

Gabe's birth rather than returning to Wellsford as she had done with the other two boys.

But then she would stop and breathe in the earthy bush smells, look out to where the sea glinted under the winter sky and dwell in the music the creek made with the wind. So much work turning the church into a home and building up a garden, why walk away from it now? Where else would she find a place so beautiful? In the end Patsy was right, she should try to work things out with Joe.

Well that worked out well, thought Lou, as she swung the Beast Machine around to park in front of Patsy's place just before ten. Inside, Marama, still in her pyjamas, was trying to light the wood-stove. Willie's deckie, Steve, was spread-eagled over the settee, the cat purring loudly on his chest. On the table an empty rum bottle held court with some finger-smeared glasses, disparate piles of playing cards, a bevy of empty beer bottles and two wax-splattered candleholders. Butts spilled out of the scallop shell on to the Jack of Hearts. Big Lou opened both doors and the window over the kitchen sink but the stale smell of booze and smoke still hung around.

"I take it your mother's still in bed," she said grimly to Marama.

The brush caught at last and a cloud of wood smoke blossomed into the room. Marama stood back, pigeon-toed, and waited until the flame had taken hold before nodding her head.

Steve gave out a sudden snore.

"With Richie," she said. "I think."

"You've obviously not had breakfast."

"No. I'm just going to make some porridge."

"Breakfast. Now we're talking," groaned Steve. He sat up, sending the cat flying, and sunk his head into his hands. "Whoa, hard night last night. A good fry-up'd go down a treat."

"You paying for it?" demanded Lou. "Ben, you clear the glasses. Nick, the ashtray and butts. Hang on, I'll take these," she retrieved the roaches. "Marama, honey, you go and get dressed and I'll make you some porridge. Steve, you can go home."

Once Marama had been fed and some order restored to the kitchen Lou sent the children off to frolic in the wild westerly, with strict instructions to take care of Gabe. She chose *America* out of the stack of tapes and settled in an armchair in front of the wood-stove with her feet propped up on the grate. The boot-line of mud on her trousers dried and crumbled as she smoked the skinny racehorse of a joint. She was dozing off, wandering through the desert on an unnamed horse, when the passage-door opened and Patsy, clad in an oversized T-shirt that barely covering her vitals, stumbled over to the table and sat there with her head sunk in her arms.

"Hard night," Lou commented at last.

Patsy nodded her head without lifting it from her arms. "You want to brew some coffee?" she mumbled.

Lou got up out of the armchair with a loud sigh. After much banging, gushing, clattering and slamming she finally sunk back into the chair again with another sigh and gazed out the window at the clouds racing inland towards the hills. Beneath the music a silence stretched between the two women, tight as a wet rope.

"You're down early this morning," said Patsy at last, squinting at Lou from the crook of her elbow.

A gust of wind howled through the eaves and rattled the iron on the roof but the silence remained, long as a desert road.

"You know I like to get on the road early," Lou snapped finally. She stood up and sprinkled some coffee over the simmering water, moving the saucepan off the heat and replacing the plate. Turning her back to the stove she flooded the room with pent-up emotion.

"It's that Aussie bastard. Oh so sweet when there's others around but I knew it'd only be a matter of time before the evil twin'd show up. Ranting on and on because the boys'd woken him up. What does he think? They're boys ... that's what boys do ... they make a noise." She paced across the kitchen to get out the mugs. "I'm sorry, Patsy. I am trying. He's okay with Gabe but with the other two … he's on their case the whole time. And then he goes into these endless rants. The only way to shut him up is to leave. So yeah, I am down here early, but where else can I go?"

"Well if you …" Patsy mumbled.

"If I what?" demanded Lou.

Patsy's head remained buried in her arms.

"Richie getting up?" Lou asked. "I suppose it is Richie in your bed?"

Patsy raised her head to nail Lou with a defiant stare. "I don't know … maybe … you want to ask him?"

"Not particularly. You want breakfast? I made Marama some porridge."

"Yeah well, you didn't have to. She can look after herself just fine." Patsy hauled herself out of her chair and slumped to the door. "Hey Richie, you want coffee?"

"Bring it in, babe," came from the bedroom.

Patsy got up and stretched. "I'll see you later," she said over her shoulder as she carried two of the coffees back to the bedroom.

"Don't forget the others are coming over. We're having our first rehearsal this afternoon," Big Lou called after her.

Such a chatter of children filled the kitchen. Ben and Thad were gobbling down cheese sandwiches and pretending not to notice Marama, Sam and Tracey whispering together on the other side of the table.

"We could easily find your stupid hut if we wanted to anyway," said Ben through a mouthful of bread. "We'll just take it over."

"Yeah, make it into a fort instead of a stupid tea party place," put in Thad.

"You'll have to find it first," sang back Marama.

At one end of the table Nick and Janey were secreting away crusts in their pockets to feed the eel. Gabe and Melissa watched wide-eyed from the other. Then, abruptly, the meal was at an end and the older children had raced down the passageway and out into the open air, leaving silence in their wake.

When Patsy and Richie emerged from the bathroom, having shared a long soak to wash off last night's grunge, the adults sat down to eat.

"I hear your suspensory loan's through," Lou said to Kate.

Melissa had climbed on Kate's knee and was running her hands over Kate's breasts while Kate was trying to butter bread around her.

"Jeez, Melissa," she snapped, laying down the knife and hoisting her on to the floor, "go and play with Gabe. Finally you have someone to play with and all you want to do is annoy me." She pushed Melissa over towards Gabe who was watching hopefully from the settee.

"Yes ... finally," she went on. "It's just as I thought, making a start on one thing meant everything else fell into place. Eddie's almost finished the plans too, now that he's been stuck out here with Jesse. He was down yesterday to pick up his mail." She spread some chutney on her bread. "This time next year I'll be in my own home, fingers crossed. Could you pass me the cheese please Mouse?"

"And what about you?" she went on after she had finished constructing her sandwich.

Lou grimaced, "Not as smoothly. Rodney's filled Joe's head with these ideas about everyone just doing what serves them best and not caring how this affects anyone else. Yesterday the Beast Machine wouldn't start and he actually demanded that I pay him to fix it. I said maybe I should demand money from him to cook his meals. 'I don't need you to cook my meals' he says. 'Any one can cook a meal.' Maybe he should give it a go sometime then."

"I guess he needs the money," said Patsy. "It's not like he can get the dole over here."

"Okay, maybe he does," seethed Lou, "but even when he does pick up some work he still expects to live off my benefit and he does bugger all to help out. We had a huge blow-up this morning. Rodney's given him a telescope, just the excuse he needs to take over the attic. So he can watch for aliens or something through that top window. I don't know what I am going to do." She took a deep breath and scrutinised the top cupboards for a moment. "Having that private space for me and the boys makes things just bearable. I can put them to bed and have some adult time in the evenings."

"Are you still thinking of leaving?" asked Mouse.

Lou shrugged and the conversation was soon taken over by Patsy who prattled on about the club last night, who was there, whom she beat at pool and who went home with whom.

After lunch Lou settled the two children down in the spare room for their afternoon nap while the other ladies took care of the domestic chores. Richie made himself comfortable by the stove and read the Saturday paper.

"What's so funny?" Patsy asked him, coming back into the kitchen with an armful of wood.

"I just love it that you Kiwis are so innocent. You think you can just declare the country nuclear-free and it'll change the whole world."

"Of course it won't change the world but someone has to make the first move," Flash Kate bridled. "We can do that, you see, because we have no real strategic value, out here on the edge of the world. We were the first to give women the vote, you know, and lots of other firsts too."

Mouse agreed. "It's like that butterfly fluttering its wings and causing a tornado on the other side of the globe. Everything's connected and so just taking a first step will bring about change."

"Doesn't matter. You don't get to decide." Richie flicked the paper back up and spoke from behind it. "I know what happens if you don't play by the rules. It's like my brother. He came back from Vietnam all angry and anti everything and now he's living on the streets and no one wants anything to do with him."

"You had a brother who was in Vietnam?" Patsy, who was charmed by all Richie's tales, dislodged the cat from her chair and sat down to listen.

"Well, half-brother really ... from my father's first marriage." Richie folded up the newspaper and tossed it on to the table. "I barely knew him. I remember he came to stay this one time when I was about ... I don't know, like ... seven and he was just about grown-up. We went down to the beach and he taught me how to skip stones. But when he came back from Vietnam a couple of years later he was really different. He got into a big row with my folks and after that my father disowned him ... haven't seen him since."

"So you don't know where he's gone?" asked Patsy.

Richie shrugged. "Still drifting around California somewhere, I guess. He's, like, a junkie. Lots of those vets are, which is my point. If you don't keep up you get left out of the game."

Mouse broke into a fit of coughing. "Even so," she gasped. "Sometimes it's better to go your own way."

"What, as a junkie?" sneered Richie.

"Well not that. That's not actually what we were talking about." Mouse, retreating to the settee, slumped back against the corner cushion and closed her eyes.

"You're right though." Patsy came leaping into the breach to defend her man. "It's not like the French are going to stop testing in the Pacific just because we go nuclear-free. I mean, yeah right, it's a noble gesture but just because American ships can't come here any more doesn't mean that anything else will change. All that in 1981 hasn't made any difference to apartheid in South Africa."

"You don't know," answered Lou, who had just come back into the room, "It's too early to tell. These things take time, you know."

The thudding of the generator dwindled away making itself noticeable by its absence.

"Lizzie will be here soon," remarked Kate.

The kitchen was awash with crosscurrents of conversation. Kate had taken over Patsy's seat by the fire and Richie was filling her in with all the gossip from the other side where most of the Play Centre mothers lived. Lou sat at the table with her head resting on one elbow. She was browsing through the paper but could not keep herself from jumping in with a question from time to time.

Patsy had decanted off a bottle of home brew and glissaded around the room handing out glasses while she raved to Lizzie, who was leaning on the bench and only listening with half an ear. Her eyes kept straying over to the settee where Paul was deep in conversation with Mouse.

"The problem I see," Mouse was saying, "is that ..." She tapped her forefinger on her knee while she gathered her thoughts. "Like, they devise these formulas, right?" She looked at Paul for confirmation.

He nodded.

"And then they go looking for it and ... there it is." Her hands spread out to display this seeming miracle. "Well ... how do they know that they're not just seeing what they believe is there?"

"Creating their own reality, you mean?" asked Paul.

Mouse nodded. Their eyes met as they pondered this proposition.

"I suppose it's because the maths follows a logical order." Paul smoothed down his moustache while he conjured up an explanation. "They extrapolate from proven hypotheses and their calculations are all peer-checked. It's not just one person's fantasy, you know. And it works, that's the thing, even if they don't exactly know why. The formula's just a way of describing an effect. The map is not the territory, you know." Paul glanced at Mouse who gazed at him in puzzlement.

"Well, you know," he went on, tracing a line on his knee. "If you look at a map of the island and follow this line, it goes from Jacob's Bay to the other side. It doesn't look that far. But we know that it is because of the hills you have to cross. And yet if you want to know how to get to the other side the map is a useful tool to show you the way, even if it doesn't capture the whole of reality."

"Mouse," Lizzie called from across the room. "Everyone's been raving on to me about your verses. I'm really looking forward to hearing them. Shall we make a start?"

Mouse looked up to find Lizzie's gimlet eyes appraising her from behind those large glasses. She swallowed, coughed a little and moistened her throat with a mouthful of beer.

"So there's a domestic scene and a bar scene," she began and went on to describe the routine, breaking off to sing the verses in a husky voice. The others joined in with the choruses.

"Oh ... that's ... that's quite challenging, isn't it?" said Lizzie once the final chorus had been sung. "Have you given any thought to how we can flip between the two scenes?"

Mouse admitted that she had not been able to come up with a solution to that. She had thought that a dolphin torch might work but it would probably be too faint.

"I guess people'll just look at whoever's singing."

"That won't work in the third verse though," Richie objected. "Everyone'll be looking at Mouse singing and they'll miss out on Kate and I." He winked over at Kate and she mouthed a kiss at him.

Patsy drained her glass and went out to the porch to get another bottle.

Mouse began tracing circles on her knee.

A particularly vigorous gust of wind rattled the roofing iron and sent smoke billowing out from the firebox.

"We've got that slide projector," Paul mentioned to Lizzie. "It's packed away but I think I can lay my hands on it."

Lizzie tittered. "Oh Paul, he's such a Virgo. Did you know that he's catalogued all our stuff so he can find anything at a moment's notice?"

"I could operate it," Paul said to Mouse under the others' laughter.

Lizzie's gaze travelled between them. "I guess that's okay then," she murmured. "So are we going to have a try-out?"

Mouse got up from the settee and looked around the room. "Um, so if I sit at the table here, you can all use the bench as a bar. I mean, the domestic scene'll be over there," pointing to the passage door, "but we'll have to work with this for the moment."

"Here, I'll just top up everyone's glasses so we have something to practice with," said Patsy.

That done they lined up at the bench. Mouse had them change position until she was happy with the balance, eventually settling for Richie in the middle with Flash Kate and Patsy on one side and Big Lou and Lizzie on the other.

"Yeah," Paul remarked. "It's like a lopsided triangle with the shorter side angling towards the domestic scene so the eye is led that way."

"That's what I thought," said Mouse.

After they had run through the routine Patsy remembered a large doll in a bassinette that she had got for Marama at a garage sale a few years back. It was exactly what they needed for the domestic scene.

"I'll ask her for it when she comes back. She won't mind. She doesn't really play with it now."

"Can't you go and get it?" asked Kate. "It'd be good to try it out."

"Fuck no," Patsy told her. "Marama never lets anyone in her room without asking. And anyway it sounds like the kids have woken up so that's all the rehearsing we'll be doing today."

Splitting Apart

We're going to be wearing leggings and t-shirts. Flash Kate went into this big rave on Saturday about how we should all wear the same and look like a proper dance troop so that's what they decided. All my t-shirts are mere rags but I felt too sick to argue. I do have a pair of leggings somewhere; it's in one of the boxes at the end of my bed … black leggings … not very exciting. Luckily Lou suggested we wear bush singlets over our t-shirts … hers are probably scruffy too… but my bush singlets have both got big holes in them. I should've listened to High Anxiety and stayed at home on Saturday. But no, carried away by Blythe Spirit's heady promises, I went along and now it's happening and there's no way I can escape.

High Anxiety's been keeping me at home ever since … although I have been sick: a cough that rasps out my throat, body aches and a head that feels like one of those medicine balls we used to throw around in phys-ed.

On Sunday a westerly was hurling rain up the valley so the girls couldn't go outside to play. They hung around inside and bickered instead. I stayed in bed reading *The Thorn Birds,* which Kate had passed on to me on Thursday, being too sick to handle physics. But after Janey had climbed up the ladder for the umpteenth time to whine at me about Tracey, I realized that I'd actually have more peace if I got up.

We played cards – first, Snap and Fish, which Janey can play, and then Last Card, to please Tracey. I made pancakes for lunch and then Tracey suggested we all draw something good that happened this week so I got out the crayons and found some paper left over from the correspondence days. She was soon deep in an elaborate map of the campground, centred around a willow tree down by the creek. Janey worked on a picture of herself feeding the eel. There was a tiny figure in the background that was Nick.

I sat on my food bin, head cradled in my hands, staring out the window at the manuka thrashing about up on the ridge. A loose sheet of iron on the long-drop clanged monotonously. The roar of the sea and the rattle of rain on the roof made conversation impossible, which was just as well because my throat felt like it'd been flayed.

Nothing good happened in the past week, observed Harshly Critical. He blew softly on his embers so that the flames flared up, seeking new fuel.

High Anxiety called me back to bed.

From his high perch Stern Discipline cast a long shadow. *You wouldn't be sick if you hadn't sat around in that wet t-shirt on Friday,* he pontificated.

I peered up, looking to Blithe Spirit for inspiration, but she remained hidden away, far above, lost in the gloaming.

The past receded on a wake of malignancy. The present shrouded me like a funeral pall. The future loomed like an impenetrable wall. So I filled my page with a black tree with ponderous boughs, thick, earth-hugging roots and very little foliage.

"That's all you can think of?" Tracey exclaimed when it came time to show our efforts. "What about all those good meals and the song?"

"I'm sick," I replied and crawled back to the warmth of my bed with a couple of Disprin until it was time to cook the next meal.

We were to have a rehearsal yesterday but I was too sick to go anywhere.

I gave Tracey a note for Kate saying they should go ahead without me and went back to bed to sleep the day away. The northwest wind came in blasts, shaking and rattling the boat-shed. I pitched about on this maelstrom through a seething confusion of visions, one barely forming before another replaced it, until the end of the day when Tracey woke me demanding to know what was for afternoon tea.

This morning the wind's swung around to the west again. The boat-shed, tucked away in the lee of the point, is sheltered from its full force but the roar flurries in my ears filling me with a restlessness that struggles to find a safe mooring.

Stern Discipline is on my case before I am even properly awake. *No malingering past the third day. The domestics are waiting.*

High Anxiety sucks me down in a spiral of despair. *This is how it's always going to be for you: alone, unloved, with a mountain of housework that'll never go away. You may as well finish it now and be done with it.*

But Stern Discipline is having none of that. *Get that kettle heated up for the dishes,* he orders. *At least the gas will warm the place up a bit. You can have a lie down once everything's straight again.*

I roll a joint to lift my spirits and smoke it while I wait for the kettle to boil. It's the first I've had since my throat got sore and I cough my way through it.

The wind comes in gusts. First there's a stirring as the turbulence approaches in the distance, rising to a crescendo as it sweeps past the boat-shed and up the hill. Then a lull while the next one builds up the energy to hurl its way through. Somewhere a tree crashes down. The iron on the long drop clangs in desolation.

Harshly Critical looks around for a good-sized log to feed his flames. *The song's going so well,* he remarks maliciously. *You really are leading the pack now, aren't you?*

You should have gone yesterday, no matter how sick you felt, growls Stern Discipline. *The show must go on.*

High Anxiety's eyelids flutter hopefully. *They've probably changed their minds anyway. Never mind, you'll be safe down here in the pit.*

A spasm of coughing tears more lining off my throat.

Yeah, just a loser, vegetating away forever, agrees Harshly Critical. *Lonely, bored ... but at least safe. You should just kill yourself now and that'll be an end to it. Nobody would miss you.*

What bliss it would be to give up this struggle to extricate myself from the bottomless pit, to sink down so deep that I never come up.

And the children? queries Stern Discipline. *Let's stop all this nonsense, straighten up those shoulders and get to work.*

After lunch I have a sponge bath and remake my bed so I can lie between fresh sheets. Out on the point waves are savaging the rocks and throwing bouquets of spray into the air. Paul won't be rowing over to feed Reuben's hens today.

So obvious you fancy him, sneers Harshly Critical. *Lizzie knows.*

How she glowered at me when Paul and I were talking about physics on Saturday. It was so scary.

Stern Discipline reminds me that I haven't read *The Tao of Physics* for several days so I struggle with it for a while, even though I'd rather carry on with *The Thorn Birds*. My eyes skim over the words without taking anything in ... something about hadrons and S-matrix theory, whatever they are. Eventually I put it aside and snuggle back under the covers, soaring on the waves of wind. I drift into a pleasant dream where I'm lying in bed with Paul ... wrapped in his arms ... his hand lazily caressing my thigh as we talk about the map and the territory.

We only notice what's relevant to the moment, he explains. *Anything else and we'd be permanently distracted. This is the map. But it's a mistake to confuse this with the territory. That's beyond our comprehension.*

But what does this have to do with physics? I ask.

So physicists are searching for a unified theory that will explain everything but, whatever they try, something is left out. Quantum theory only goes so far before it runs into the constraints of relativity. Every theory they come up with is a map to one aspect of the territory but the whole remains elusive. There's always something more.

The howling wind fills my head. This whole physics thing frustrates me to hell. All those hours of concentrated reading and I'm more confused than ever. His arm encircles me and I sink into his side like butter into hot toast.

You can always change your map, he murmurs into my hair.

Then he's pulling me on top of him, his knee forcing its way between my legs and rubbing against the tiny nub of sensitivity that hides there. My loins dissolve. My legs split wide apart. I open myself up to him. He is plunging, plunging inside of me, driving a primal cry up, up, to burst out of my raw throat and mingle with the battering wind. The cry pulses into a scream as I ride out the waves of ecstasy until I subside into a molten pool, there, beneath the covers.

Later I wake from a deep sleep. The girls will be home soon and I should be getting up but my body is an immoveable mass. It's best I just stay here until the very last minute: warm, comfortable, sated, enclosed in the sound of the waves flinging around shingle as they churn over the boat-ramp below me and the wind-thrashed trees above.

But there's someone knocking at the shed door.

At first I think it's just something loose being worried by the wind but then the door opens and the duel between wind and sea intensifies.

High Anxiety freezes my body. *Just lie still. No one'll see you up here.*

I meld with the mattress and hold my breath.

But then Big Lou calls out, "You there, Mouse?"

A visitor! You see someone does care about you. Blithe Spirit emerges from wherever she's been hiding these last days.

I throw back the covers and scramble down the ladder with Harshly Critical's voice booming in my aching head. *Caught malingering. What a weakling she's going to think you.*

But Big Lou's not here to judge me. She's just come to see how I am. The girls are going to stay up with Flash Kate for a while to give me a break. We chat about the weather and other incidentals while I make a pot of tea. I tell her about the course of my illness and we agree that it's best to be up and about on the third day.

Once the tea things are all laid out ready I sit down opposite her. I'd like to ask her how the rehearsal went but I notice that her eyes are fixed on her lap where she is weaving the bottom of her jumper between her fingers. She obviously has something she wants to tell me. They've probably decided not to do the song after all.

"I'm … that is… I've left Wairua." The words burst out of her. "For good this time," she adds abruptly.

I twirl the teapot around and back again, pour the tea and hand her a cup. "Are you moving in with Dutchie?" I ask, cautious because I don't think this is it.

"Well, no. Didn't you hear? Dutchie was flown off Sunday morning. The McLaren boys beat him up real bad at the Fishing Club on Saturday night."

Naturally I'm shocked to hear this but not really surprised. Everyone knows that it was only a matter of time. He never could leave well enough alone. Lou tells me that they say his jaw might be broken and a cracked rib or two.

"So … obviously not meant to be," she goes on. "Probably for the best because I doubt it would've worked out. He lives even further out than Wairua, so it'd be even more of a hassle getting the boys to school. And all that moaning would be hard to take. I don't know about the sex either. I mean … it's not like I've slept with him or anything but … you know … if you don't have it, you don't have it … simple as that. So … probably for the best, eh? Horse Fly's moved in there to keep an eye on things until he gets back."

"But why leave now?" I ask. "Has something happened?"

I wave my dope tin in her direction and she nods gratefully.

Her fingers resume their weaving motions. "I just can't be up there any more. Let's just leave it at that. I'm going to stay with Patsy until after the ball and then …"

Her gaze is on some distant place. She sucks at her lips to hold back tears.

I light the joint and hand it to her.

"It's such a mess!' she exclaims once she's had a toke. "You know, Mouse, what it's like to put your soul into something and then have it all turn to custard, how hard it is to admit that you've failed and to walk away. And where can I go, a solo mother with three young boys to care for?" She straightens her back – these food bins are notorious for making you slouch – and watches me drawing down on the joint.

"We're leaving the Island altogether. I can get a job somewhere ... use my training. We'll go back to Wellsford first, even though I don't get on with my old man. I don't have enough money to set up anywhere else."

She takes the joint back and has a puff. Her shoulders slump again.

"The boys don't want to leave. They love it here. But I've had enough. I want a washing machine, electric lights, something to do with my life that's not taking care of fucking men.

"I'm just waiting on the Universe," she concludes with a brave shrug.

We sip tea and pass the joint between us until she's ready to tell me what happened.

"It's that bastard Joe's fault," she burst out on an expelled breath. I"d even agreed to move down into the doss-pit so he could have the attic as he wanted. All day Sunday moving everything down there and bugger all help from him. It's not bloody fair. That attic was put in for the children to have a place to sleep away from the rest and when everyone else had left I'd come to think of it as our private area. But no. Patsy told me I should let him have his way to keep the peace, so I did."

I nod sympathetically and take her cup to refill it.

"That bloody track last night ... so muddy and the wind howling through the trees! I kept telling the boys that we would be home soon, home to a nice warm fire. Instead, darkness. No fire lit, the wood box empty and Joe nowhere to be seen. Of course, once the food was finally ready to be dished up he comes sauntering in expecting to be fed."

"And then, all night, tramping up and down in the attic, hour after hour. Meanwhile I tossed and turned and worried. You know how all your grievances come to the surface in the wee small hours."

She thought she had a handle on things but when she got back from dropping the boys off at the school bus there he was sitting in the kitchen reading amongst all the unwashed dishes.

"I just couldn't control it," she told me. "It seemed like a lifetime of anger, anger I've been holding down forever, this torrent of it, erupted out of me.

'Fuck you,' I screamed, 'when are you ever going to do anything to help out around here.' I was throwing dishes into the sink. So angry!"

He had just sneered at her anger. "That's what the government's paying you for," he'd said. "To keep house."

Lou shakes her head sadly. "That's when I knew that we had to leave. So I told him that. At first he didn't get it. 'Yeah', he said, all conciliatory. 'It'll be easier for you down there, closer to the school and all your lady friends. You're obviously not happy here, with all your constant whining and demands.'" We exchange a knowing smile.

"But when I told him I was leaving the island altogether," she continues. "Ooh he was so angry. He came and stood over me, grabbed hold of my shoulders and threw me back against the wall. My head bounced off the door jamb so hard that stars sparked. There's a huge lump there." Her fingers work through her hair just above the start of her plait. "Then he stormed out and I haven't seen him since. Poor little Gabe was hiding outside in the bush. I just bundled up a few things we might need and left. We can't go back. I can't stay in a place where I don't feel safe," she concludes with a deep sigh.

No word about taking Game away, notes Harshly Critical, snidely. *That could be relevant, don't you think?*

But what can I say? How could she even consider that when her hatred of Aussie Joe is so acrid? Even moving out of the attic was a huge concession for her. And, anyway, I'm not meant to know.

It's all your fault, Harshly Critical reminds me, raking over his embers. *This wouldn't have happened if you'd gone to the rehearsal last night.*

"I feel really bad making the rehearsal yesterday and then not turning up," I say. "If you hadn't gone out to that at least you would've been saved the trek back in the dark. I have been really sick though," I add.

It's starting to get dark here in the boat-shed. I get up and find a candle to light. We sit in the glowing circle, listening to the incessant wind.

"How did it go anyway?" The words are lightly spoken, carelessly, as if it doesn't really matter.

Her hand, a broad capable hand calloused and reddened by hard work, smoothes the table top. "Actually ... Patsy and Kate've had a bit of a bust up." Her eyes meet mine across the flame. "They don't want to do it any more."

Harshly Critical throws brush on his embers. *It's fallen apart. Wouldn't have happened if you'd gone to the rehearsal last night instead of malingering. Well it's too late now. It's over! Of course you were really stupid to think they'd do this with you anyway.*

Back to the pit, High Anxiety murmurs smugly.

I get up to clear away the tea things so I can concentrate on keeping my voice steady and unconcerned. "What ... what did they fall out over,"

"Oh you know," says Lou airily, "men. Kate found out ... well Richie told her actually ... that Patsy'd had an abortion when she was in town. He reckoned he was all upset because it might've been his, but it could just as well have been Pete's ... or some other guy whose name Patsy doesn't remember. I don't know why he had to tell Kate about Pete. He's such a gossip, that guy. You never know what he's going to blurt out next.

"But anyway, Kate went right off the deep end. She came steaming around yesterday, purely to have it out with Patsy. After all there wasn't much point in having a rehearsal without you. They had a big slanging match and now they're not talking. Kate's a bitch really. She doesn't care about how bad things have been for Patsy. It's all about Pete. And here's me caught in the middle as usual."

The food bin scrapes back and she stands looking down at me. Her jumper's hand-knitted, brown, home spun. There's a red darn level with the candle flame.

"I'm sorry, Mouse," she says. "It would've been fun but what can you do? Men eh? They spoil everything."

The loose iron on the long-drop clatters forlornly. I wish she'd hurry up and leave so I can be alone.

"Well, best be off. You rest up and stay warm now. You want to be better for the ball, eh?"

The door opens on the confused whirl of wind and surf and closes again, muting it to a dull thrum in the background. I'm left to sit alone at my table.

High Anxiety makes herself comfortable in the bottom of the abyss. *No one can harm you if you stay safe in here,* she assures me.

The walls of the pit press in around me as Blithe Spirit howls, wailing out of the isolation and despair that I'll never escape.

Loser, screams Harshly Critical. *Getting ideas above your station. Thought you could be a star did you? Someone's been smoking too much wacky-backy, I'd say. May as well put an end to it now.*

The darkness thickens around me until Tracey and Janey come running down from Flash Kate's place, trailing their school bags behind them. They stand at the open door looking at me. The candle flame wavers in the draught.

"What's the matter?" asks Tracey. "Why haven't you started dinner?"

"I'm real hungry," says Janey, even though I know she will have been filling up on Kate's baking.

Stern Discipline stirs himself. *Pull yourself together and get those kids fed. It's only a song after all.*

"There's nothing the matter. Close the door before the candle blows out."

The muscles on my face take on a happy expression. I light more candles and the girls sit at the table and chat about their day while I cook dinner – boiled potatoes and onion mashed up with butter and milk and sprinkled with chopped parsley from outside and the last of the cheese.

Tracey's not fooled however. Once the potato soup's ready she interrupts Janey's story, about a girl she was reading with today who's her next best friend, to ask me once again what the matter is.

"Oh it's nothing." I dole the soup out into three bowls and hand them around. "The others have decided not to do the song, that's all."

"Why not?" she demands. "It's because you didn't go to the rehearsal last night, isn't it?"

"It's just some adult stuff," I tell her. "It doesn't matter. It wasn't much of a song anyway."

The girls spoon up their soup. I stir mine around ... clockwise, then anticlockwise.

Tracey pushes back her empty bowl. "So ... what? You're just giving up? After all our practising? You've got to go and talk to them. Tell them they have to do it."

"It's sweet of you to be concerned, honey," I tell her, "but that's not how things work in the adult world. They've got their own reasons." I start clearing the table and for once she jumps up to help me.

"Like what?" she asks.

"Just adult stuff. It doesn't matter," I say again.

The evening routine takes forever. Tracey has spelling words to learn and Janey, a new reading book. There are hot water bottles to fill and bedtime stories to be read. It seems that it will never be over. But finally they're asleep and I can return to my refuge in the loft and reach out for the sustenance the *I Ching* has to offer. I count out the sticks through the dammed-up tears misting my sight and the cry in my throat that aches for release.

The Corners of the Mouth offers me nourishment. It tells me to be temperate in eating and drinking and to pay heed to what others fill their mouths with. There is one moving line. The first one:

You let your magic tortoise go,
And look at me with the corners of your mouth drooping.
Misfortune.

The words swim through my unshed tears. I cannot believe that the *I Ching* could be so mean! The hexagram moves into *Splitting Apart.*

It does not further one to go anywhere.

At least the wind's loud enough to drown out my crying, for tears fall long into the night and I wouldn't want to disturb the girls.

Hanging in Limbo

When her feelings threatened to overwhelm her, Patsy Dervish found it soothing to perform a cleansing ritual. The crystals lined up on her kitchen windowsill marked important events in her life. Belle had first given her amber to strengthen her attitude when she ran away from home. The citrine, a symbol of happiness, marked Marama's birth. She got onyx to give her persistence when she moved over to the Island and on and on. The latest was turquoise to help her rejuvenate after the abortion. On Tuesday, after a strained evening in front of the stove with Big Lou, she ha d gathered up her crystals and left them outside in a bowl of rainwater to absorb the light from the waxing moon. Once the housework had been done the next morning, she dried each one individually with a silk cloth and ordered them in a new pattern. Van Morrison crooned in the background.

Lou had gone to visit Flash Kate again. She reckoned that Gabe needed someone to play with to take his mind off what had happened. Yesterday she had leapt up as soon as Marama came home from school saying, "Oh fuck, I forgot about the boys," and hurried off to collect them from the wharf where the bus dropped them off, which was fair enough, but then she was gone for hours. She reckoned that she had gone down to tell Mouse the song was off but Patsy knew that she had been getting from Kate all the comfort that Patsy herself was unable to give. For Patsy's loyalties were torn.

Pete had brought Aussie Joe back to Thames with him when he had returned from looking for land on the Island. Of course, as a foreigner, Joe was unable to buy land on an offshore island outright and so he was keen to become a shareholder in Pete's land company. At first it had been just Pete, Joe and Patsy building the dream, although, by the time they moved in with Lou, they had become quite a crowd: both shareholders and hangers-on. It did not take long for Patsy to notice that Joe was obviously besotted by Big Lou. He would drop what he was doing to drive her anywhere and spent hours getting her clapped-out old Triumph moving again. Patsy couldn't resist teasing him but he was such a strange, lonely guy, taken up with obsessions from all the books he read. He never could compete with Tom, who could worm his way into any woman's bed.

When Gabe had been born, and questions about his parentage festered below the surface, Patsy hoped that Joe's gentle soul might prevail. But even when Tom was long gone Lou remained resolute and Patsy watched Joe's love turn to bitterness. This latest craziness worried her. It was not like Joe to turn violent. She really should go up and see if he was all right but she wouldn't because she was hoping Richie would come back.

No one noticed when Richie had slipped out on Monday afternoon, after Kate had stormed in, all riled up and foaming at the mouth. Patsy was furious with him. What was he doing spilling out the very secret she did not want Flash Kate to know? There are limits to how much one should gossip, limits to do with loyalty. And then to slink off without even explaining himself ... and yet ... and yet her bed felt empty without him.

She was telling Big Lou all this yesterday when Lou remembered her boys and rushed off to get them. Even later, once the children were in bed, Big Lou was of little comfort. Clicking away self-righteously with her knitting needles she said Patsy should forget about Richie because he was never going to stick around. He was a drifter, island-hopping across the Pacific on his father's purse, and sooner or later he would head on back to the States. Patsy was just fooling herself thinking he would take her with him, however much she thought she loved him. Lou paused to count her stitches. She seemed about to say something else but merely added that these things were sometimes for the best.

Of course, Lou did have problems of her own but Patsy would help her with those because the Island without Lou was beyond imagining. When Lou first came bursting in with wild tales of battery, she was all for fleeing the Island for good on Friday's boat. Patsy persuaded her to stay for the ball, to take the two weeks until the boat returned to find another solution. Dutchie would be back by then and maybe she could move in with him. Or Lizzie might know of a place she could rent. And there was Pete; he'd sort Joe out when he got back.

Patsy stood back to admire her display and selected a crystal to carry around with her: a yellow topaz to attract beneficial influences.

Big Lou had an urge to stamp her foot at Patsy, as if she were an old ewe and Patsy the sheep dog trying to pen her. It irked her that she had given in to Patsy's pleadings and agreed to stay for the ball when she just wanted to leave the Island behind her for good. It wouldn't even be that much fun now that Patsy and Kate were at each other's throats. And what if Patsy got her to change her mind over the next two weeks? The last thing she needed was to get stuck here for another eight years.

Gabe, confused by the ugliness of the day before, clung to Lou with all the tenacity of a paua to a rock. Ben and Nick carried on their lives with careless abandon but she could feel them watching her from beneath their sandy lashes, waiting to see what she was going to do. If they were to have any stability at all it was time to cut her losses and leave, to retreat to Wellsford until she found the new direction the *Tarot* had been talking about.

That morning she had lain in bed going over her finances while she waited for everyone else to wake. Mouse must have sold some weed in town, because she had paid back the loan as soon as she returned, but money had flowed out while they were staying at Patsy's. There was barely enough to pay all their boat fares, so going earlier by Sea Bee was out of the question. She wondered if she should ask her father for money but the thought of his gloating squashed that idea fairly quickly. And she doubted if any of her friends had money to spare. She wondered if she would last the distance with them all cooped up in Patsy's spare room, Gabe tucked in beside her and the two older boys top and tailing in the other bed.

Over breakfast that morning Patsy was still going on and on about Flash Kate.

"It's not like the bitch owns him or anything," she said, waving her porridge spoon to emphasize her point. "When we get right down to it she had thrown him out. Why shouldn't he keep me company? We're mates, after all."

Seeing Ben pause, with his spoon halfway to his mouth so as not to miss a word, Lou tried for a change of subject. "Ah well, she'll get over it. What're you wearing to the ball?"

"Something so provocative that Pete'll find me irresistible. I'll show that bitch. At least I won't have to watch her flaunting around with that loose-lipped Richie on her arm any more, now that this song isn't going ahead."

Marama pushed her bowl away and swallowed the last of her Milo. "You got to decide soon ... ball's only two days away. And what about me? What am I going to wear?"

"You kids aren't going," Patsy replied. "I've already told you that. Lizzie said 'no kids'. It's to be a strictly adult affair."

"But that's not fair!" protested Marama. "How come you adults get to have all the fun and I get left here with these dumb boys?"

"I don't care. Dancing's for girls." Ben declared. "We can take care of ourselves."

"You'll have a babysitter, of course," said Lou. "If we can find someone, that is. If we can't then we won't be going either. We'll be stuck here with you kids," she added with a wry smile.

"A babysitter for Gabe, yes, but not for us," argued Ben. "We're not babies any more ... well Nick too maybe ... he's still a baby and a girl baby too ..."

Nick punched him and they grappled with one another until Lou got up from her chair and pulled them apart.

Patsy took out the makings and rolled a cigarette. "You'll be having your own special time here," she told them. "Thad and Melissa, and Sam'll all be staying ... Tracy and Janey too probably. You can stay up as late as you like and we'll get in some ice cream as a special treat."

"Where're they all going to sleep? Not in my room ... well, Sam can sleep in my room ... and Tracey too, if she comes ... but not Janey. She's a baby. Maybe she could sleep with Nick ..." Marama smirked. "Only now you're not doing the song they probably won't come. Tracey says Mouse doesn't like going out." She stood up and grabbed her bag.

"I'm off. You boys coming?"

Patsy Dervish and Big Lou went over the babysitting options once again as they did the morning chores. Lizzie was relying on the teenagers who did their high schooling by correspondence to babysit, but the days had slipped by and she had been too preoccupied with her own affairs to ask any of them. Now they were already committed elsewhere.

"Perhaps Lizzie should do it since she's the one who says there's to be no children. Maybe she'd find out what life's like when you don't have a honey like Paul to do all the domestics for you," Lou said bitterly.

Patsy cleared the last of the dishes off the table and wiped it down. "What about Mouse? Marama's right, she really doesn't like going out much. And now we're not doing the song ..."

"That hardly seems fair." Cutlery rattled around in the sink. "We could ask her, I suppose," Lou went on as she began fishing out the cutlery with the pot scrub. "After all two of the children are hers and I'll bet she hasn't asked anyone. She does just drift along and leave everyone else to make all the arrangements."

Outside clouds sailed across from the northwest playing peek-a-boo with the sunlight that had crept down the valley as far as the washing line.

"Good drying day today," Lou noted. "Thankfully that wind's dropped a bit. It was really doing my head in.

"For fuck's sake, Gabe, let go of my leg!"

Gabe, who had been clinging to Lou's leg while she washed the dishes, gave a howl that turned into an inconsolable tantrum. The cat jumped off the settee and scuttled under it with flattened ears.

"Gabe, Gabe, look you're upsetting the cat." Lou gathered him up and sat by the stove, rocking him and murmuring, "I'm sorry. I'm sorry."

Gabe screamed on and on, struggling against her, until she lost patience and thrust him into the passage to scream himself out. Patsy turned up the radio and they danced their way through the dishes until he calmed down and Lou could take him outside to hang the washing on the line. He stood next to her, silently handing up the pegs. The wind sported with the clothes, tossing them about as she pinned them down.

Aussie Joe's furious face played over in her mind. His brows were arrowed down over his eyes, his mouth was wide with shouted obscenities. She felt again the grip of his hands on her head, the bang, bang, banging against the doorjamb and remembered how Gabe had cowered under the table in the vestry, peering around the corner, ducking back whenever Joe turned his way.

He had thrown her aside like a used rag and disappeared into the bush. She was left to sit at the table in the vestry nursing her throbbing head, body wracked with sobs. Gabe stood beside her, stroking her arm and murmuring comforting words.

Finally she had pulled herself together and stuffed as much as she could fit into her pack, grabbing this and that without even thinking clearly what they would need, and set off down the track with Gabe without a backward glance.

"Mummy." Gabe broke into her thoughts. "Will we ever see Joe again?"

She never wanted to see that bastard Joe again. She cringed when she thought of him, the way he was always undermining her authority. Did he think she was not capable of disciplining her boys, the way he leapt in to take Gabe's side against the other two even when Gabe was being an annoying little shit and well deserved what they dished out to him? It had been obvious, those few days when there was only Gabe up there with her at Wairua, that he genuinely cared for Gabe and she had begun to soften despite her misgivings. She remembered him carrying a laughing Gabe on his shoulders up the track, mock wrestling with him on the double mattress in front of the fire, the gentle jibbing over breakfast. Back then she had started to believe that they could work out it out. But after the other two boys returned she had come to see that admitting even the slightest possibility that Joe was Gabe's father would have him taking over their lives completely. Lou did not feel up to the battle.

She looked down at Gabe's anxious little face. He was holding up a peg and waiting for her to answer. Not yet three. Did he understand what Joe had said to him about being his father? If they went away and he never saw Joe again would he even remember him? She took the proffered peg and pegged up a pair of Nick's trousers.

"I like Joe," said Gabe firmly. "He's my friend."

"Yes, well..."

In silence she hung out the last of the washing. Gabe handed her the pegs, one by one. The clothes flapped in the wind against the drone of the morning cars coming and going and the ever-present thudding of the generator.

"Tell you what ..." she said to him as she took the last peg, "how about we go around to Kate's and see if Melissa wants to play?"

Kate was out underneath the puriri tree, stripped down to leggings and t-shirt, chopping wood. Her rhythm did not waver even though she must have heard the Beast Machine swinging around and parking in front of her place, and Lilith giving a short bark and rushing up the path with her tail wagging, Up the axe swung and down into a chunk of wood so large and dense that the axe-head stuck fast. She bashed the wood against the chopping block until the axe loosened, turned it over, and swung the axe down into it across the previous cut. Once again it stuck so she upended it and slammed the back of the axe into the block. The wood sprang apart into four pieces. Melissa scurried forward with her little wheelbarrow and loaded up a piece to wheel it away the wood-box beneath the kitchen window.

Yesterday had been a cleaning frenzy fuelled by tears. Today, anger. With any luck, thought Lou, by the time Pete got back she would have worked through every emotion and have realized how trivial it all was.

"After all, if Richie'd kept his mouth shut the whole thing would've been forgotten and no harm done," she had said to Patsy during last night's bitching session. And, when Patsy's hostile stare reminded her that the abortion was not something she was ever likely to forget, added hastily, "Well, you know, to Kate that is. "

Kate moved over to the wood-heap and picked out a bit of wood with a large knot running through the middle of it. Sweat ran down her face. She lifted the bottom of her t-shirt to wipe it away.

"How's that cheating bitch Patsy this morning?" she snarled.

Lou glared at her. "Look, I don't want to talk about her ... that's between you and her ... I won't be dragged into it. It's not like it meant anything. It was just a trivial one-night stand. As I understand it you'd thrown Pete out anyway."

Flash Kate started splitting off wood from around the knot. "Of course you would take her side." Thunk! "But then I suppose you don't have any other option now that you've left Wairua." Thunk! "Maybe I should take Aussie Joe's side against you."

Lou stood there, stewing. 'For fuck's sake', she felt like shouting. 'My problems are way worse than yours. My life's been turned upside down. Just because one harvest moon, out of it on mushrooms and sucked dry by life, I allowed that Aussie bastard to lure me down to the swimming hole to undergo a so-called 'sacred union' with him. How could he ever have thought I'd give up Tom for him? Wasn't it enough that I called the boy Gabriel, giver of light, to please him, even though Tom'd always named our boys? Why couldn't that have been enough? Why couldn't he have just left us alone?'

Lou waited until Gabe, who had taken over the wheelbarrow, was over by the wood-box out of earshot. "Kate," she hissed, "he told Gabe he was his father. Told him, just like that. How dare he!"

"Well, isn't he?"

"No he's not! Just because Gabe's got dark hair like me doesn't mean I've been having it off with a fuck-wit like that."

Kate selected a smaller straight-grained length from the heap. The axe hung in the air. It crashed down splitting the wood in two. She kicked them aside.

Melissa ran to pick them up. "Gabe, It's my turn now. See I've got these two bits to put in."

"He's not!" Lou insisted again, one eye on Gabe who was wheeling the barrow down from the wood-box. A stubborn expression darkened his brow.

Kate turned back to the woodpile. "Y-e-ah, right," she answered dismissively.

A hacking cough broke through the hostile silence. Mouse was emerging from the flax bushes. She was so breathless that Kate had divided a sizeable round into six before she had recovered enough to speak.

"Hi," she rasped.

Kate drove the axe down into the chopping block. "So you're out and about again, are you? Well, I guess you'd both better come in for a cuppa."

While Kate completed the domestics, and saw that the children had their lemon drink and Anzac biscuits under the puriri tree out of the wind that buffeted the deck, the niceties of weather and health were covered. Mouse, flopped down into the chair facing the kitchen, her head propped up by one arm, the other slung carelessly over the back of the chair, gave an account of her recent illness. Her breath rattled as she drew it in.

"It's a pity we're not doing the song but I guess you must be pretty pissed off with Patsy," she said when Kate was settled at the table with them.

Kate lit the cigarette she had just rolled and glared at the other two women through the smoke. "You don't know the half of it," she exclaimed. "I know when it would've happened. Easter right? The kids had gone over to spend it with my folks, no doubt so they could fill their heads with all that Christian nonsense." Her eyes narrowed against the smoke and she stared out through the ranch-sliders at the tousled ocean.

Mouse gazed at her in sympathetic silence.

"You know what it's like," she went on. "Finally you have the place to yourself, you go to a lot of trouble, not to mention expense, so you can enjoy some time alone. I bought a chicken to roast for the two of us, with apple pie and cream to follow, persuaded Rose to sell me a bottle of rum from the Fishing Club, put out flowers and candles and fresh sheets on the bed." She dragged on the cigarette one last time and savagely stubbed it out.

"And?" Mouse prompted.

"Well, you know ... it was only going to be a couple of drinks at the Fishing Club and then he'd be right over. But then someone was going over to the Surf Club and, of course, he couldn't disappoint him. Never mind about me. He rolled in at some ungodly hour of the morning, pissed as a fart. Of course I threw him out. What would you do? And so he runs off round to Patsy's place and jumps into bed with her. And she, the bitch ..."

She got up to rattle loudly at the fire grate and thrust more wood into the flames. The children's happy laughter floated in from outside. A chainsaw whined in the distance.

"And the next day he takes off to deliver that timber and bring your stuff around, Mouse. He bounds up the track three days later with some scallops he'd dived for on the way back, all repentant and 'it won't happen again' type of thing. You know how they are. Hard to say no to."

"Still, it's not Patsy's fault," objected Lou. "She wasn't to know. And it's been hard on her too ... having the abortion and all."

"Yeah, well I guess I have that to be grateful for," snapped Kate. "Although she probably would've nailed Richie with it had she kept it."

Mouse reached out for an Anzac biscuit and took a thoughtful bite. "Did Patsy go up to the Surf Club with him?" she asked.

"What? I don't know. I don't think so. What's that got to do with it?" Kate stared at Mouse.

"Well you've just said how persuasive he can be. And if Patsy hadn't had any for a while she would've found it hard to say no. I mean, obviously Richie must have come into the picture after this. It's actually Pete you should be angry with."

A crumb caught in her throat and she was taken over by a coughing fit. When it was over she rested her head in both hands and breathed heavily for a while. "I must say I'm rather disappointed that some man stuff would be more important to you than the sisterhood. This was a chance for us ladies to create something, something about us, our story, our song. And why are we not doing it? Because of some bloke who couldn't keep it in his pants."

Flash Kate leaned forward and pinioned Mouse with a stare of icy burn. Every word was clearly articulated. "I will not perform with that bitch. Never! Yes, she's right, I don't own Pete. But I will not have him sneaking off to sleep with her. God only knows what diseases she could be carrying the way she sleeps around." She sat back in her chair and began rolling another cigarette.

"In the end this 'nobody owns anybody' is just so much bullshit. It only leads to trouble. I'm not the only one. We, all of us, are jealous at heart. So easy for a slag like Patsy to think it should all be free love and just follow your instincts. She'd think differently if she ever found someone she really cared about. We all want to keep a tight hold on what's ours, even you Mouse."

Lou nodded in agreement.

"And anyway, Mouse," Kate continued, "you didn't even bother to turn up for the rehearsal."

"I was sick," Mouse snapped. "It was just one rehearsal ... you could've carried on without me. It's not like I haven't been practicing at home." Once again she was overcome by coughing. "How hard is it to sing the chorus, prop up a bar and cozy up to Richie?" she gasped. "I'm sure you've had plenty of practice."

She rested her forehead on her hand and sighed.

Lou went over to the sink and brought her back a glass of water.

"I've always envied you ladies ... how you help each other out," Mouse went on after she had had a sip of the water. "Remember when we went to find your boundary pegs the other day. You didn't think twice about asking Patsy to look after Melissa. Neither did she think twice about agreeing even though she probably had other stuff to be getting on with. You ladies do that for each other. Do you really think that Pete or Richie or any other man would've taken care of Melissa like that? Oh yes, they may've done the work for you ... something they could take all the credit for and would be paid for in some form or another. But childcare? Not likely."

"Yeah, right on Mouse," cried Lou in a burst of enthusiasm. "The sisterhood forever!" She held her coffee mug aloft and Mouse clicked it with hers.

Flash Kate glared at them. She swilled down the last of her coffee.

"Let's just have one more rehearsal tomorrow afternoon," Mouse begged. "See how it goes."

"I doubt the bitch'll agree. And what about Richie? He slunk out of there the other day like a dog who'd stolen the Sunday roast."

"Patsy'd be in if we could get Richie back," said Lou. "I think he's the one she'd forget free love for. Surely you must feel for her over that. We all know he's not going to stick around."

Kate smirked and rattled her fingers against the table edge in a rapid tattoo. She began gathering up the coffee cups. "I suppose we could call in and see him on the way home from Play Centre tomorrow. You'll come to Play Centre tomorrow, won't you?" she asked Lou. "You never know, you might find someone over that side who knows a place to rent."

Lou's brows came down to veil her eyes. She snorted and shook her head slightly but suggested they take her car.

After the logistics for this outing had been sorted Flash Kate agreed to give it another go, seeing as it obviously meant so much to Mouse. "But don't think for a moment that I'm going to be friendly with Patsy Dervish," she warned Mouse. "She better stay out of my way."

Mouse swilled down the last of the water and stood up. "Good. That's all I ask." She gave them a smile, festooned with the cobwebs of some dark inner space. "The tide's out so I'm going to take a wander to see what the sea's washed up. I'll go around Jacob's Bay way and call in on Patsy ... make sure she's okay with it."

Big Lou stayed for lunch and a game of Scrabble. Nothing much was said about Mouse's visit until near the end of the game when Lou, musing on six vowels and a D, asked, "What do you think's brought on this sudden burst of assertiveness? It's not like Mouse at all."

"With Mouse? I dunno, maybe she's getting a bit."

"Really? So you think there's something to Lizzie's suspicions? They certainly seemed very chummy on Saturday. This'll have to do," replied Lou putting down 'adieu' on a double word for a score of 12.

Kate leapt in to put down 'quell' with the 'q' on a triple letter. "That's 34," she crowed. After she had added up the score she continued, "He did drop in a few weeks ago. He's lent her this book about physics – really dry stuff. She must be besotted with him to even bother reading it."

"Patsy says they were seen cuddling over by the wharf last week."

"Last week … oh yes, he did row her back from the wharf … Wednesday it would have been. She'd been drinking with Old Tom and wasn't here when the girls got back from school. I don't know anything about him cuddling her though. I mean, what would the attraction be? No, I'd say it's all pretty harmless."

"Is it just about the song then? It obviously means more to her than we thought. It's certainly rather gutsy of her to get up and sing in front of everyone like that, especially as her voice is … well … it's not that great, is it?"

Oh well, we'll just have to humour her, I suppose," said Kate. "That's the last of the tiles."

Before Completion

'm working from a new map now. On Wednesday morning I woke
up without my magic turtle – the song that was going to transform my
life – and I felt quite bereft. But then I realised that it's the mapmaker
who chooses what will go on a map: what the perspective will be. I
needed to change my map. I needed to stop looking at the particle
and consider the wave.

So I burnt the dragons. Once the girls had left I took out all my
drawings of the abyss and arranged them on the kitchen table. I lit a
candle and placed it in the centre, its glow pale against the gloomy
morning light. One by one, I took up the dragons, tore them into
strips and held each strip over the candle flame. Over and over
the flame flared up as the paper singed and curled, and died away.
Finally only a circle of powdery ash lay around the burning candle.
A lingering smell of scorched oil from the pastels hung in the air.
One long puff blew out the candle and blew the dragons out of my
mind, their ashes mingling with the dust in the room. Then I cleaned
and tidied, had a sponge bath, washed my hair and dressed in fresh
clothes, I was ready to go out and fight for my song. The last two lines
of the Image in *Splitting Apart* says that 'those above can ensure their
position only by giving generously to those below.' So I went out to
offer all I had, which was a listening ear.

After leaving Kate and Lou, I wandered along the beach to

visit Patsy. I found her huddled in her armchair beside the stove strumming sad songs on her guitar. On the hearth beside her the scallop shell overflowed with butts and the home brew jug stood empty. She jumped up at the sight of me and siphoned off another bottle. "Grab yourself a glass," she said, all gaiety. She poured us both a glass and chatted away about inconsequential things as we took our seats in front of the stove.

"I'm so sorry to hear about your abortion," I said gently. "That must be so hard. "Well that opened the floodgates. Her eyes brimmed with tears as she told me how it had all come about.

She never could find the right contraception. The pill made her fat and quite put her off sex, which kind of defeated the purpose. She had to have the IUD removed because it became dislodged and was causing her so much pain. And forget condoms because what bloke's going to agree to wear one. In the end it had felt easier on her conscience to do without altogether, relying as much as she could on keeping track of her monthly rhythm. "Catholic guilt. It's a heavy burden to bear, you know," she told me. "As much as I try to bury it, it's never entirely forgotten. And now I've had an abortion, which is worst of all, all because Easter turned into one of those 'never rains but it pours' type situations: three fucks in one weekend, would you believe it?"

The last one was Richie. She's fallen in love with Richie. He's so wonderful. She has some rather fantastic dreams for the future. I think she may have been watching rather too much TV while she was in town.

"But now that bitch has driven him away," she concluded sadly as she topped up my glass. This gave me the opening I'd been looking for. She listened agreeably enough until I had mentioned that Flash Kate and Big Lou were going to Play Centre together the next day.

"Oh, so Lou's going off with her again tomorrow, is she?" she huffed. "Maybe she should move in there, seeing as they're such great mates."

Not even the plan to get Richie back over here placated her. As she saw it that just gave him more reasons to visit Flash Kate and gossip about her.

"Just like Lou'll be doing now," she snarled.

"Lou wouldn't do that," I'd pleaded. "She's just trying to distract Gabe from, you know ..."

Well this opened up a whole new can of worms. She filled me in on Lou's history with Aussie Joe, which, well, has shown me quite a different side to things. We were tossing around some ideas to keep Lou with us, even though I'm pretty sure   she wants to leave, when Lou, herself, arrived back, carrying in a sleeping Gabe. The conversation turned to more general things and I left shortly after. I needed to get back to the boat-shed before the girls got home from school.

That evening I vowed to not smoke another joint until I've done this thing, to give my cough a chance to heal. I've hidden my tin in the rafters out of sight but the image of it floats like a familiar at my shoulder. I'm constantly tempted to clamber up on a food bin and get it. And of course the dragons didn't go quietly. On Wednesday I was too taken up with other people to miss them but yesterday, Thursday, they seeped back. High Anxiety's faint wail from the floor of the abyss whined through my lonely thoughts. Harshly Critical gnawed at my confidence. I kept having to remind myself that they'd never been apart from me: that their thoughts were my thoughts and that I was in control.

It's hard. Yesterday morning I wanted a joint so bad that I lingered over breakfast hoping that I'd yield to temptation. Finally, when no more tea could be dredged from the pot, I went outside and lit the fire to distract myself despite the saturated clouds drifting across from the northwest. It was a struggle to keep it going until there were enough embers to heat the camp oven. I had to cover the fire with a sheet of corrugated iron every time a shower went across and then take it off again a few minutes later. But we needed bread. The girls had taken chapattis to school for lunch all week because I'd been too sick to light the fire. It was easier to mix up flour and water, give it a quick knead, pat it into rounds and cook it in the frying pan. Yesterday, though, Tracy had refused to take lunch if she had to take chapattis again: or 'hippie bread' as she sneeringly called it. So I'd had to search around for some money for pies.

All morning, then, while I was taken up with domestic chores, I persisted in keeping the dragons at bay and the tin tucked away in the rafters. It was a relief when afternoon came at last and I could leave it all behind and skip from rock to rock around the point to go to rehearsals. Paul had rowed back from Rueben's in plenty of time for Lizzie to join us and we walked up the beach together. I told him that I'd nearly finished *The Tao of Physics.* He's going to drop by and pick it up next week sometime. How Lizzie glared at me when we entered the shop together. She bustled me over to Patsy's place before I even had a chance to say goodbye. Not that there's anything for her to worry about. All we ever talk about is physics. And yet ... maybe next week when he comes to visit...

At rehearsal we found Patsy Dervish sulking by the fire. Flash Kate was planted in the chair nearest the door, rigid as iron and her nose aiming for the ceiling. Big Lou hovered between them making sandwiches for the children who had slept in the car all the way home from Play Centre and were fractious. Occasional remarks were being lobbed at her from either side through the stony silence. She rushed to greet us as if we had came bearing a pitcher of water for a dehydrated soldier, rather than a flagon of port. How difficult it is being caught between two warring parties. No wonder Lou wants to leave. I feel for both of them but more for Patsy, who's been hiding the grief for a lost baby beneath a frivolous mask. After all, who wouldn't give in to some man slipping between your sheets during the witching hours? Not if it was someone you loved and it'd been so long since you'd lain in a man's arms.

It seemed like all my efforts to reconcile them had been useless.

But once the port started flowing and Richie bounced in, full of energy and enthusiasm, there was a thaw and we managed to run through the song without incident. Flash Kate and Richie made us all laugh the way they flirted together. She was in high spirits when we finally left for home. She offered us dinner and baths after the dress rehearsal tonight.

I'm standing out on to the point, my back to the sea, arms outstretched, leaning against the wind. My hat's off so the wind can blow through my hair. The moon's in Capricorn and Saturn's going direct. The moon calendar says it's time to move ahead with plans. There's lots of coming and going over at the wharf. The boat's just docked. Collapsing waves litter the sea. A rogue one swamps the rocks where I'm standing and I leap out of the way just in time. There's a yacht tacking across the bay. Further out another one races before the wind. I suppose one of them will be Pete coming home. Kate came down this morning to tell me that he'd caught the outgoing tide, although with more foreboding than joy. He'd have made good time with the wind behind him.

It felt strange having Flash Kate to visit. Usually she calls down for me to come up, or sends Thad with a message. I was hanging out my sheets, fresh-washed from the sweat-drenched days of sickness, when she guided Melissa out of the flax. The tide was on the way out and the oystercatchers were pottering along like two old women, probing for food with their long orange beaks. Lilith sprang down the beach to scatter them then poked around where they'd been to see if there was anything worth eating.

"Melissa's so excited," Kate gushed. "Aren't you, honey, excited because your Daddy's coming home?"

"He's bringing me a present," Melissa said. One hand kept a tight hold on Kate's leg, the other cuddled the fox-skin stole Patsy had given her. "You're excited too aren't you Mummy?" she asked uneasily.

For all Kate's reassurances, Melissa sensed that something was wrong. I found her some toys to play with over on Janey's bunk and fluttered around making us all hot drinks.

"We won't come up for dinner tonight then," I said to Kate, who was perched on the very edge of her drum as if she was scared of catching something.

"Of course you must come." Kate glanced at Melissa. "Why wouldn't you?"

"Oh, no," I protested. "You'll be wanting family time. We wouldn't want to intrude."

In a low voice, born in the icy reaches of the south, she insisted that Pete would not be getting back into her bed that easily. "Although," she added bitterly, "he's probably been getting all the company he needs over there on Waiheke."

I didn't really know what to say to this so I asked her if there was a babysitter lined up yet. She shook her head doubtfully. There was a pause while she concentrated on rolling a cigarette. When it was done she lit it and said through a mouthful of smoke that she supposed one of us would have to stay behind if we couldn't find anyone.

Melissa was chatting to the fox-skin as she threaded it through a dress she'd found. Kate smoked her cigarette. I fiddled with my mug and longed for a joint.

"You're not really that keen on going out, are you?" she asked after a time. "Do you want to do it? We could pay you. Of course it would mean dropping the song..." She left the phrase to dangle in the air.

For a brief moment High Anxiety surfaced, offering me an opportunity to back out of the song, to take back the dragons and return to life as normal. But I reminded myself that she no longer existed, that any anxiety is mine to master. It seemed incredible that Kate would even suggest this, after all that had happened, but it was only fair in a way. After all I'd made no attempt to find a babysitter. I thought of how excited the girls are about staying at Patsy's place.

They had chattered away about it over breakfast this morning while I put together their vegemite sandwiches and listened to them with half an ear.

"Marama's only letting Sam and me sleep in her room," Tracey had said through a mouthful of porridge. "We're not letting any boys or little kids in."

Not that Janey cared. "Nick says I can top and tail with him in the boys' room. Ben says it's okay because I'm almost a boy anyway."

"Pooh," returned Tracey, "Who wants to be a boy? Just because you tagged along after them when they took over our hut last night."

They had still been going on about it when I thrust them out the door to catch the school bus. I hadn't had the heart to tell them then that there was still no babysitter. I've searched my mind for someone I could ask but I don't know anyone.

"I really want to do the song," I quavered. "But ..." It'd been no small effort to get us all together again. My eyes travelled around our little shed looking for a solution.

"Perhaps we could do the song early and I could take over afterwards," I suggested at last. "One of the others could stay with them until then."

Of course Kate was quite happy with this because it won't be her, or Lizzie either for that matter. It'll probably be Big Lou because she's leaving anyway, which makes it worse somehow. I must say I'm disappointed. Kate says not to worry, that something will turn up, but I have my doubts.

"What about your costume anyway?' she asked airily. "Are you going to wear that dress Patsy gave you?"

"It doesn't matter now, if I'm going to be babysitting."

I have a great idea for my costume but I don't want to reveal too much before the day. Besides I was feeling a bit sulky. After all it was my big night and I was going to be shuffled off as soon as my song was over. I won't get to bask in my glory and there won't be a chance to even dance with Paul. It's so unfair. But, there, the song's the most important thing and at least I'll get to do that.

Anyway Kate went on at length about how I could still do my grand entrance and that was what counted at a fancy dress ball.

"That's what everyone remembers," she cried gaily. "No one cares how you look after that. Have you tried walking in those heels?"

Well I had, once or twice, but I couldn't do it without wobbling. I'd pretty much given up on wearing them. However Kate insisted I should and gave me some severe coaching until I could stride confidently down the boat-shed and back with barely a tremor. Once she was satisfied she took Melissa home and I heated up the remains of last night's lentil soup for lunch.

What a patchwork of light and shade there is in the wave. I read the *I Ching* to try and make sense of it all. It was just *The Well*. No line. No other hexagram to help me interpret the meaning. Just sending down the bucket and hoping I've done all that I can to prevent the rope from breaking or the bucket falling short of that clear, clean water. I turn my face into the wind and imagine Paul's lips caressing mine. I feel enclosed in it, as if I'm enclosed in his arms. I'm transported out of my mundane, mousey self to some higher being, clothed in flowing robes, strolling with him beside a murmuring brook, discussing arcane thoughts. We lie down on a carpet of daisies. I pick some and make a daisy chain to crown him. His long fingers tilt my face up to his. His moustache tickles my cheek as his lips brush mine.

We travelled in uneasy silence around to the wharf just before five. It was already getting dark and the headlights swept across the ridges of gravel thrown to the side of the road. Old Gert hummed and rattled. Her tires swished over the wet road. The children huddled together on the back seat. Kate was in a dark mood. No one dared to upset her with idle questions.

I'd come in from the point and was taking the sheets off the line when I heard the sound of Pete's outboard pulsing into the bay. He'd given me a cheery wave and called up that he had got me a transistor before he disappeared into the flax. I'd completely forgotten that I'd given him a small bag of dope to swap for a radio. That'll help keep the dragons at bay.

Before I'd even taken the last sheet from the line angry voices had echoed down the hill between wind gusts. Then he had come striding down again, had gunned the outboard and had cut a path through the incoming tide towards Jacobs Bay with not one glance back at the A-frame.

The hall lights were already on. Reuben had arrived back today too. He and Paul were joking away together while they set up his stereo and gave it a sound trial. Soon we were all dancing to the music, yahooing and laughing. The hall echoed with the shouts of children chasing each other around the pool tables and sliding across the floor in their socks. It really felt like plans were indeed moving ahead.

Lizzie was happier than I've seen her in ages. Paul's staying at Rueben's place tonight so they can get an early start in the morning to unload the cladding on the full tide.

"No time now and we'll be in," she laughs. "Paul wants us to wait until it's completely finished ... he's such a Virgo, needing to have everything perfect ... but I'm determined to move in as soon as it's closed in."

Patsy Dervish also bounced in, full of good cheer because she'd solved the babysitting problem and also, although she didn't say this, taken the first step in persuading Lou to stay. Dutchie came back on this morning's Sea Bee. He has a cracked rib, which makes moving difficult, so going home just yet is not on the cards. Patsy's insisted he stay with her in the meanwhile. She's even given up her double bed for him and moved into the sunroom.

"He may as well babysit since he can't dance," she said, "and I won't have to feel guilty about leaving the exchange unattended."

Lizzie looked a bit grim at this. Flash Kate's told me that she hates how cavalier Patsy is about the exchange but Patsy just laughs when she mentions it.

The first obstruction came when we'd changed into our leggings, t-shirts and bush singlets and came out of the ladies' toilet to find Richie still lounging around in his usual jeans and jumper. I hadn't even thought about what he'd wear. Kate offered to lend him some leggings and almost come to blows with Patsy over it. But Richie was not fazed. He reckoned his costume would do the trick but it'd have spoiled the surprise if he'd worn it tonight.

I move restlessly beneath my duvet. A streaky cloud drifts over the moon and casts a shadow on the sea. He says to trust him but what if he looks all wrong? It'll be too late then to put things right.

We had to stand around for ages while Paul and Reuben tried to get the projector working properly. When they put it on a table, the beam was too high to capture any more than the faces of the chorus line standing at the bar. And the children, who had lined up some chairs to form the audience, broke off their fidgeting, nudging one another and exchanging insults, to complain that they couldn't see past it. Paul suggested trying a chair next but that was too rickety.

While the other ladies hung around making useless suggestions, I edged closer to the door, fighting the urge to make some excuse, to run home and leave it all behind me. It felt like madness thinking that this would work. But then Reuben brought in a couple of beer crates from out the back that did the trick perfectly. We all took our places.

Apart from Richie and Kate, the others don't really have a lot to do beyond singing the chorus and propping up the bar, which is really only a hatchway through to the supper room made for handing out cups of tea and coffee. You wouldn't have thought there'd be a problem but none of them have been practicing. Lizzie doesn't even know the words.

And nothing fits. The bassinet and the doll are ridiculously small and all the teapots in the supper room are huge. I'll have to take my teapot along, I suppose.

And do you think Paul could get the order for moving the projector right? Of course not. We had to do it over three times and even then I'm not sure he really understood what he was meant to be doing. Even the prospect of having her house finished wasn't enough to stop Lizzie from getting snappy.

And then there's the friction between Patsy Dervish and Flash Kate. Just before our last run through Rose came in to set up for the Fishing Club. The chorus line insisted that it'd be more realistic if they had liquid in their mugs so everyone bought a beer. During the first chorus, Patsy waved her mug way too vigorously and drenched Kate. I'm sure it was just an accident but Kate broke off flirting with Richie ... I must say they do look well together ... and, had Lou not dashed off right away to get a towel to dry her off with, there'd have been another stoush.

After we'd linked arms and step, step, step, kicked our way into the passageway by the supper room the children all gave a cheer. I was happy to leave it at that but Rueben murmured something to Paul and he reminded me that we needed to come back in again for the bow.

"Maybe come back doing the gumboot dance and the chorus again and then bow," he suggested. So that's what we're going to do.

In bed, now the rehearsal is over, I turn towards the window and stare into the bright night. A streak of silver reflects the nearly full moon from a pool on the empty beach. I'm excited, scared, quietly confident, all at once; too churned up to sleep. Did we work out all the problems at the dress rehearsal? It's not a big thing. It should go off all right. But there's so much that could go wrong. The waves are dying down and only the odd splash of foam shines phosphorescent in the moonlight. I wish I could feel so calm. I turn back to face the darkness of the shed. The words of the song revolve around my mind like an endless record. Panic consumes me. What if they don't like it? What if they think it's really stupid and they don't even clap? I toss and turn. There're wrinkles in the sheets and my feet are cold. Why I ever went along with this I'll never know.

The Ball

Lizzie is too young to remember the time the community rose above their petty feuds just long enough to build a public hall. For her it has always squatted beneath the hills beyond the wharf: a monument to pragmatism amongst the swirling fecundity of nature. What they wanted was a space for weddings, funerals, public meetings, Anzac Day celebrations, Christmas parties, the odd dance to keep the womenfolk happy and, especially, a place to gather for a drink or two. So it is not a building of any grandeur, no celebration of the architectural arts. Having learnt through years of depression and war to accomplish the task with whatever was easiest to come by they built a rectangular box of concrete blocks to enclose a space that does the job it was intended for. No sooner had it been declared open than the Fishing Club was formed and it has presided over the building ever since.

The moon has not yet worked its way above the eastern hills but the sky is clear and pinpricked with stars. Lizzie is trying out a few Charleston steps in the empty parking area while she waits for Paul to start the generator. She had found her flapper dress in the Cook Street Market a few years ago but has never found an occasion to wear it until now. She loves its silky feel and its muted green colour like the underside of a flax strand. It goes well with her cloche hat of forest green that keeps her rampant hair in check, although the hat presses her glasses down on the bridge of her nose so she doubts she will wear it all night. The puce tights add a definite touch of craziness. It's a pity her only respectable shoes look so battered, and are not even heels, but her grandmother's amber beads and her long ebony cigarette holder add a nice touch. What a shame she will not make a grand entrance and instead will be stuck behind the table collecting the cover charges. It's always her who has to do the hard yards.

All day she has been rushing around: up at dawn to help with the unloading of the timber and to make sure the men have a good breakfast afterwards, then over to the airfield to pick up the papers, then busy in the shop all morning with everyone out to vote, then up to the school to vote, then round to the hall to check on the decorations, then home for dinner and to get ready before dropping Sam off at Patsy's. And still there was more to be done: the trestle tables had to be set up in the supper room and covered with table-cloths from the kitchen, the float had to be checked, the pool table moved to the back of the hall and the chairs set up around the walls.

At least Patsy Dervish and Big Lou have done a good job of the decorations. The Wairua boys cut a load of nikau fronds to cover the walls and her sister has done well at Geoff's Emporium. Not only has she sent over blue and black crepe paper for streamers and a packet of white balloons but she has also found some rolls of holey aluminum – the waste product from the manufacture of milk bottle tops. When the lights are turned on it is like being in a bushy glade beneath a night sky with twinkling stars and a full moon of balloons.

"Isn't it magical!" she calls to Paul. It takes her breath away how handsome he looks in the sailor suit Reuben brought him back from town, so tall and slender in the hip-hugging pants and tight red-and-white striped T-shirt.

"Look at those muscles," she says, reaching out to touch his biceps. "All that rowing was good for something after all."

But there is no time to stand around if they are to have the hall set up before people start arriving. Rose, in a blaze of burnt orange and crowned with sun-rays, arrives to take care of the bar. People drift in. The hall hums with conversation as they catch up with what has happened in each other's lives since the last public occasion.

Patsy Dervish stops at the table to pay for herself and Lou. She is muffled in a long woollen coat. "Where's the music?" she complains. "I thought Reuben'd be here by now."

Lizzie stifles a moment of panic. "He'll be here. He's very reliable."

"Fuck that." Patsy drops the coat and gyrates over to the bar in the skimpiest of bras and harem pants so low-slung that they threaten to fall down altogether. Somehow she has fastened a cluster of diamantes in her navel that sparkle as she rotates her hips in time to some beat only she can hear. Lou has followed her in carrying their plate: stuffed eggs covered in a tea towel. She exchanges a smile with Lizzie as Patsy gives a special wriggle towards a couple of fishermen who are standing by the bar goggling at her.

Big Lou is wearing an outrageously short nurse's uniform. Her fleshy thighs bulge out between the straps of the suspender belt that holds up her white stockings. She has gathered her hair into a topknot and stuck it through with a giant hypodermic needle cut out of cardboard and covered in silver paper.

"Already quite a turnout," she says to Lizzie, scanning the groups of animated chatterers. "Anything needs doing?"

Lizzie sends her to set out cups and saucers in the supper room. The tables are already filling up with a variety of finger foods: chocolate, carrot and banana cakes, sausage rolls, stuffed eggs, raw fish, chips and dip, home-made cheeses and a range of different slices. A group of serious-minded men huddle around a radio in the corner.

Reuben finally arrives. He is a stocky, heavy-set man, dark and hairy, and has kitted himself out in studded leather for the occasion. Always taciturn, he merely grunts at Lizzie when she mentions the time and swaggers over to the stereo to start up the music.

Mouse totters in on her high heels. She takes a jittery glance around the hall then abruptly drops her gaze to the table. Lizzie sees that she has noticed Eddie, spivvy-sharp in a gangster's pinstripe suit with Angel hanging on his arm as his moll.

"Don't worry," she reassures Mouse. "You look brilliant."

Mouse does look terribly elegant in the red dress. She has highlighted the black tights and black high heels with a red bow around her left ankle and counterpointed it by a necklace of jet-black beads. Lizzie has no idea what she is meant to be but is impressed nevertheless.

Paul gets it however. Mouse gravitates towards him as the only friendly face she can see. He surveys her and nods appreciatively. "Yin and yang, eh?" Mouse twirls around in front of him and they share a private smile.

"Look at them smiling at each other?" Lizzie mutters to Flash Kate. "And you say there's nothing going on!"

"They're just friends," Kate shrugs. "For god's sake don't go upsetting her before we've got this song over with."

She strides out on to the floor, majestic but dangerous as The Black Widow. Her bodice is so tightly fitted that her breasts threaten to spill out of it and, just in case they have been missed, she has dangled a gold crucifix just above her cleavage. Her legs stretch out endlessly in the black tights and black leather boots. Scarlet lips pout out of a whitened face framed by her blonde curls. She wields a single red rosebud like a weapon. The men gathered around the bar follow her with their eyes. In a far corner of the room a lonely pirate smiles sadly into his beer.

Rueben puts on Split Enz and cranks up the sound, drowning out the conversations. Patsy Dervish takes the floor. She is joined by a gypsy woman, who has come over from the other side, and a witch, come down in a group from up north. They circle one another, swinging out over the floor and then twirling back to circle once more.

Mouse stands at the back of the hall swinging to the beat and gulping down a beer to steady her nerves. Finally she can resist no longer, swills down the last of the beer, lays aside her glass and sways on to the floor. As the pace picks up she casts her heels aside and loses herself in the music.

Ah, the language of the dance, a churning mass of colour and movement: groups split up and merge again, two dancers share a special beat, then fly apart to mingle once again with the crowd of gyrating forms.

Most of the men are yet to join the floor. They stand around yarning, beer mugs in hand, watching the dancers out of the corners of their eyes. But gradually they stand up with their partners. And as more couples come on to the floor the dance takes on a different nuance: secret glances are exchanged over shoulders, seductive moves are executed just outside of a line of sight. The surging beat drowns out the few people still catching up with one another and the whole hall surrenders to the dance.

At the end of the second bracket of music Richie drifts over to Mouse. Oh how elegantly louche he looks in his rumpled white linen suit and Panama hat. He raises one eyebrow at Mouse and she nods enthusiastically.

Patsy joins them, a glass of whiskey in hand. "When're we doing this thing?" she asks. "If you leave it too late we'll be too trashed."

Mouse is poking around beneath the chairs for her heels.

"Now?" she asks once she has mounted them.

"If we're going to do it at all," Patsy agrees. "I'll tell Lizzie and you round up the other two. We'll meet in the toilet. And we'll meet you," with a seductive flutter at Richie, "in the supper room when we've changed."

Before the others have even begun undressing, Mouse is already in a green t-shirt, yellow leggings and her bush singlet. She slips through the supper room and out to the porch to extract her gumboots from the pile at the door.

Regardless of what she wore at the dress rehearsal, Flash Kate has decided to leave on her leather boots to get out of wearing gumboots.

She pulls a red T-shirt over her bodice and covers it with a bush singlet. Her white face is streaked with sweat so she occupies the space in front of the mirror to wipe it off and redo her lipstick.

"I must say Richie certainly looks the part," she says to Patsy and Lou. "Like a regular bar fly."

Patsy weaves back and forth, trying to get a glimpse of the mirror over Kate's shoulder. Her leggings are striped in orange and yellow and her t-shirt is orange. With her ginger hair she looks more like a bee than ever.

"I think he looks beautiful," she replies. "Do you have to hog the mirror?" she snaps.

Kate wipes her lipstick off again and, slowly, deliberately, begins to reapply it. She pouts thoughtfully at her reflection.

"Come on you two," says Lou. "We've got this far. Don't start fighting now." She has opted for paisley leggings and a pink t-shirt. Her bush singlets were all full of holes so she has gone to the trouble of darning the least holey one in a rainbow of colours.

"She's such a slag," pronounces Flash Kate haughtily. "Heaven knows what diseases Pete's caught off her."

"You fucking stuck-up bitch," shouts Patsy. She grabs Kate's mass of blonde hair and pulls her head away from the mirror. "No wonder Pete's off all the time. He can't wait to get away from you."

Kate has hold of her wrists, trying to get her to let go of her hair. When this is unsuccessful she elbows her in the stomach, leaving Patsy bent over and gasping for breath. Kate turns back and rearranges her curls in front of the mirror.

But Patsy is not done yet. She leaps at Kate, clawing at her face, and Kate is just in time to grab her hands and force them above her head. They dance around one another.

Lizzie bustles in. She is running late, as usual, but expects that the others will be ready already and she can have the room to herself. Instead she finds the small space around the toilet consumed by a writhing mass of female fury. She looks across at Lou, who is calmly hanging her nurse's uniform up carefully on a hanger, but she merely shrugs and turns away.

Kate steps forward and grinds down on Patsy's bare toes with her leather boot.

"Bitch,' screams Patsy, hopping out of range. She forces Kate backward into the toilet until she falls onto the bowl and has to let go of Patsy's hands to regain her balance.

"For fuck's sake cut it out," exclaims Lizzie.

"Yeah," adds Lou. "You better not let Mouse catch you fighting."

At this moment Mouse rushes in, full of nervous energy.

"Aren't you lot ready yet? Come on, I've got everything set up and Paul's announced us. Come on, come on, everyone get in your places. Lizzie, aren't you even dressed yet?"

Lizzie hurries to get changed. Patsy flounces out to get her boots and Kate rearranges her hair once more. A buzz of anticipation filters through from the hall as people find good vantage points around the walls and Paul sets up the projector.

Even when Reuben turns off hall lights the buzz continues. The light from the supper room casts the group at the bar in outline and a thin projected beam picks up Mouse, sitting at the table with a teapot and mug in front of her. The bassinet is just visible behind her. She pours some tea, takes a sip and begins to sing. As her voice gains volume the conversation stops and her plaintive, slightly cracked voice prevails.

Alone again,
Oh the pain,
No more wanted as a domestic slave.
I have my own worth,
Of that I am sure,
But how can I find it
In a do-mestic chore?

The light swings to the bar. Fortunately Mouse is too immersed in her role to notice that her carefully balanced line has gone askew: Lizzie having judiciously taken Kate's place to keep some distance between the warring parties. They merrily sing the chorus, swinging their beer mugs to the beat.

Oh we skip through the trees,
With the greatest of ease,
First on our bottoms,
Then on our knees.
The dishes aren't done
And the beds are unmade,
And all life is,
Is a pattern of shades.

The light stays on the bar. The audience watches Kate move past Lou and snuggle up to Richie. They watch Richie fawn over Kate. Mouse continues her lament.

He left me
For another.
Just didn't want
To be his mother.
We have our own worth,
Of that we are sure,
But how do we find it
In a domestic chore?

The ladies sing the next chorus, while the light follows Richie and Kate over to the table. They cuddle together, totally absorbed in each other. Behind them Mouse slips over to join the others at the bar. The audience watches Richie sitting at the table, reading the newspaper, while Kate rocks the baby with mounting agitation. Mouse is singing from the bar:

Now he's had
A baby again.
She leaves him
To feel the pain.

Kate's anger has reached a crescendo. She thrusts the baby in to Richie's arms. The audience catch a glimpse of him looking in bemusement at this tiny bundle but the light moves quickly off him. It follows Kate stalking off to the bar where Lizzie hands her a mug of beer and they all raise a glass. All the while Mouse sings:

He has his own worth,
Of that he is sure.
Maybe he'll find it in a domestic chore.

Arm in arm they sing the chorus again, step, step, step kicking out the door. There is silence for a moment and then a burst of laughter and applause. Then nothing ... Paul rushes behind the scene but returns shortly after and clears away the projector. The conversation surges back and the place where Mouse sang her song is soon washed away as everyone crowds in to have supper.

The women are talking about the song. The younger women crow triumphantly but one of the older women leans over to a friend from the Women's Division and asks, "What was that all about?"

Her friend shakes her head, "Some hippie thing, I guess," she whispers back.

Most of the men were too busy gawping at the sight of flashing legs to really listen to the song but one mutters to his mates, "You know how to keep a woman?"

His mates chorus back, "Tied to the kitchen sink with a chain to the bedroom." They all guffaw and crowd the bar for another drink.

Mouse has refused to go back for a bow. She tears off her leggings and hurriedly pulls her on red dress. Lizzie changes quickly too and hurries out to take control of the supper. Mouse carefully reties the red bow and takes a quick glance in the mirror to check that her jet necklace is correctly aligned. Kate catches her eye in the mirror.

"Wow, Mouse, I never thought you'd go through with it. Hey girls, we did it! We really did it!"

In that moment all animosity is put aside. They throw their arms around each other and dance manically around and around in that tiny space until Mouse breaks away and scrabbles in her backpack.

"I've got to have a joint," she gasps. "Any of you in?"

"I'll be out in a minute," replies Lou. Kate and Patsy are more intent on another drink.

Mouse slips out into the Hall, gumboots in one hand, joint secreted in the other. She notices Angel and Eddie, deep in conversation at the back of the hall. Angel glares at her but Eddie doesn't even glance in her direction. As she passes the bar some fishermen snigger.

"Hey chicky, you can be my domestic slave anytime you want," one calls after her.

But there's Paul leaving the hall. He'll be glad to share a joint with her. She moves towards the door after him but people are coming up to congratulate her and talk about the song so, by the time she gets outside, Paul has already disappeared.

A shower has just passed over. The puddles in the car park glint in the full moon. Over there, in the shadow of a van, two people are kissing. The bulkier of the two is laying the other back against the van. The very physicality of them sends a pang of desire through Mouse's loins. She has to squeeze her legs together to keep it contained. She looks away, up at the moon sailing between the gathering clouds.

But there is something so familiar about that slender silhouette abandoning itself to the other. She draws back into the porch and flattens herself against the wall, looks again to be sure. Waves crack sharply along the beach, suck out, build up and crack again. The generator churns out a steady beat.

Yes it is Paul.

Mouse draws a deep breath, blinks back tears and peers out once again. The moonlight glints on silver chains.

Reuben.

It is Reuben and Paul, together there, in the shadows.

"Do you want to go to my car?" Lou asks beside her.

Mouse feels the cold wall against her palms. The two men have sunk out of sight. She draws in a deep breath.

"Let's go over to the wharf and have it there. It's so lovely out here in the moonlight," she says.

The sea ripples around the wharf piles beneath them with quiet murmurings. The moon casts a sheen of light across the harbour. Their hair is ruffled by a slight breeze. Mouse wishes she had her coat.

"How're you feeling now it's all over," Lou asks.

Mouse sucks on the joint to cover her confusion, the song submerged beneath another matter entirely.

"I can't believe we even did it," she replies on an out-breath. "It seems totally unreal. What was that all about?" she asks of the moon.

"It's certainly got people talking," Lou says taking the joint.

"Maybe," answers Mouse. She looks longingly over to where the boatshed lies hidden beyond the point. If only she could be in her loft now, safe amongst her dragons.

"How're things with you anyway?" she asks to change the subject.

Lou is leaning over the wharf rail immersed in the movement of the water below. "Just enjoying the evening," she replies. "Tomorrow? I'll tackle that tomorrow."

The music starts pumping again, drowning out the chugging of the generator. The joint passes back and forth between them. The next cloud is smothering the moon and a few drops splatter on their bare arms.

"Best get back," says Lou. "It's starting to rain."

A sombrero supported by two short legs approaches Mouse as she weaves through the crowds of dancing couples.

"Haven't seen you for a while," says Old Tom. "How about a dance for old time's sake?"

Surrendering once more to the rhythm, she dances with Old Tom; dancing, dancing, to drown out her conflicted feelings. Horse Fly grooves by in pink and green jockey silks and she turns to dance with him for a while before turning back to Old Tom. The floor is a single organism, pulsating with movement.

"One bourbon," they cry, stamping their feet.

"One bourbon, one scotch and one beer."

Paul dances by. He whirls around to share a beat with her.

"Great show," he yells in her ear and smiles encouragingly at her. A smile floods her face until she remembers. She turns back to Old Tom. They dance on together until the music finally stops and she can gather up her things and follow the white moonlit road home.

News filters through from the supper room that Muldoon has conceded. Reuben puts on *Poi E* and the floor erupts. Everyone bellows "*Poi E*" in time with the music and a space clears in the middle of the floor to give Rose's youngest room to do his break-dancing moves.

"Things are going change now," shouts Lou to Rose. "We're going to build a better, more inclusive society and show the world how it's done."

"We hope, girl, we hope," replies Rose.

Aussie Joe sidles up to the bar. He has made no effort to dress up.

"Give us a whiskey, Rose," he slurs.

Rose serves him without comment.

He gulps down the whiskey and moves closer to Lou. "You think you can keep Gabe all to yourself, don't you? You think you can just take him away and I won't ever see him again. It's not right!" He glares up into her face with a manic glitter in his eyes. She takes a step back, out of range of his alcoholic breath. "You can't take my boy away from me," he goes on. "He knows now. That's not something he's likely to forget. Keep looking over your shoulder, you fat bitch," he snarls as he walks away.

"That's one angry man," Rose says to Lou.

Lou shrugs and sips her rum and coke. "What can he do?" she asks. But her heavy brows close down over her eyes and she finishes her drink in silence.

"Isn't this great?" Lizzie yells to them above the music. "I've pulled it off. Everyone's having a great time. You not dancing Lou?"

Lou downs the last of her drink. "I don't know. Something's not quite right. I think I'll head home now and check on the kids. We shouldn't leave Dutchie alone with them for too long. Can you give Patsy a lift home, Lizzie?"

"Sure," replies Lizzie.

"Can't leave him alone," she laughs to Rose as Lou hurries away.

She plunges back into the crowd, grabs Paul's hand and glides around him to the slow beat. "You look so handsome, my sailor man," she calls to him fondly but he does not hear her, does not take her in his arms, barely seems aware of her. He's gazing at someone over her shoulder as if he has reached the end of the rainbow and found there all he ever wanted.

She turns around to see who has attracted such rapt attention. Reuben is leaning against the wall in his leathers, smoking a cigarette. He thrusts his hips in time with the music.

"No," Lizzie gasps. Realisation swamps over her like a rogue wave. "Oh no, it can't be."

Paul starts out his trance. He looks down at her.

"I'm sorry," he mutters. "I'm sorry, I'm sorry, so very sorry,"

Couples have taken over the floor now. They dance by locked in one another's arms.

"I'm sorry," Paul says again and shrugs. "It's just who I am." And he turns and walks away, walks across the floor to Rueben.

There are dishes to be washed in the kitchen, surfaces to be wiped and tablecloths and tea towels to be gathered up to take home to wash. It is as good a place as any to hide when your world has changed forever. Lizzie wonders how she could have been so blind, how they could be such bastards, how long they have been carrying on like that under her very nose.

And what about my house? she considers as she folds up the tables in the supper room and stacks them back against the walls.

"You alright, girl?" Rose calls across to her.

I must keep up appearances, she tells herself. *This is my night, my triumph and I won't let those bastards take it away from me.*

"You got any tequila?" she calls back. "The night's over now. I'm going to get plastered."

It is the end of the night. The dance floor has emptied. Only the last minute hook-ups remain.

Kate dances alone in a corner. Her courage fails her now. She lets her rosebud slip from her grasp and coasts over to the bar to get a final drink. A rangy pirate with a patch over one eye picks it up and follows her to return it. He draws up close behind her and holds it in front of her.

"Oh Pete," she whispers, turning into his arms. "I've missed you so much."

They melt together and stand, swaying to the beat.

"I do love you, you know," he offers.

Patsy watches them over Steve's shoulder. Richie avoided her all night and went home with the gypsy woman from the other side so she has had to settle for Steve. She snuggles against him and he grips her arse in both hands, pulling her crotch against his hardness.

Contemplation

It's the Saturday morning after the ball and Kate and I are sitting in the patch of sun outside the boat-shed enjoying a coffee while we watch our children play down on the beach. While I've been in hiding all week she and Pete have been clearing her house site. Patsy's been looking after Melissa and Aussie Joe's been helping out too. Pete thought he needed taking out of himself now that Lou's left the island for good.

This is Kate's first big news. Big Lou went home early from the ball. She'd had a sudden premonition that something was wrong. Just as well too, because Dutchie, slowed down by his cracked rib, had missed two calls within half an hour of each other. When Lou got there he was waiting in the exchange to see if they called again and shortly later her stepmother called to say that her father'd had a stroke. They had a whip-round and got enough money together for her to leave with her boys on Sunday's Sea Bee. They're all going up to Wairua this afternoon to pack up the last of her stuff so it can go on the boat on Friday.

Richie's disappeared over to the other side. No one's seen him since the ball. At first Patsy was in mourning, with Lou having left as well. But Kate thinks things have started to develop with Dutchie. They're always sitting around the kitchen table when she calls in to pick up Melissa, knocking back the home brew and laughing together. She doesn't think they've done it yet, Dutchie's ribs are still slowing him down, but they seem very happy together.

"Odd," I say. "I wouldn't have thought he'd be her type."

"Neither would I but, you know, Patsy's always needed a protector and now Lou's gone ... And it's good, you see, because for once she's had to get close to somebody before jumping into bed with him."

She balances her mug on the bank beside us and rolls a cigarette.

"There's something about Paul too." She squints at me through her cigarette smoke.

"Paul?"

"Don't you know?" She has difficulty keeping disappointment out of her voice. Maybe she thinks I have some inside information to share. "Lizzie's thrown him out. He's moved in with Rueben. We thought it was over you. Lizzie was sure there was something going on between you and him."

"Ah, no." Laughter catches in my throat and I go into a coughing spasm. "He just lent me a book."

Paul did call in yesterday to collect *The Tao of Physics*. I haven't been able to shake off my cold so, every day, once the girls had left for school, I huddled back in my bed and lay listening to the radio. It seems that the country is on the verge of bankruptcy so all this economic stuff has suddenly become very important and I've been trying to make sense of it. Fortunately I noticed him rowing ashore so had enough time to scramble down from the loft and pretend I was clearing the dishes before he came to the door.

I greeted him calmly and continued rinsing and stacking to give him space to talk. He stumbled a bit but gave me pretty much Kate's account of things. He's going to stay with Reuben until the house is finished and then ... they'll have to see. I could've told him I knew the truth. I was tempted even to play with him, to appear surprised and ask him probing questions as to why? and when? and for how long? But I decided to accept the map he's working from. It's his business as to when he shows us a more accurate one.

"Anyway, why haven't you been out?" he asked me. "Everyone loved the song. They're all talking about it."

"My cold got worse," I said, "and I haven't felt like going anywhere."

Actually I'd been battling with myself all week. My moment in the spotlight was ruined because I lost my nerve before the final hurdle. The rope broke and the clear water remains undrunk. I'd been too ashamed to even read the *I Ching* until that morning and even then I didn't feel like following its advice. *Contemplation* is about going out and contemplating the world, about seeing and being seen. The Judgement says:

Contemplation. The ablution has been made,
But not yet the offering.

And this is so true because I sang my song but then I didn't stand out there in front of everyone and take my bow. Instead I ran away and hid and I've been hiding ever since.

There was a line, the third line:

Contemplation of my life
Decides the choice
Between advance and retreat.

I'd been thinking about this when Paul arrived so when he suggested I go with him over to the shop I agreed. I wondered if there was any mail and it was benefit day on Tuesday so I could draw out some money. Besides, we were running out of food.

The hexagram moves to *Development (Gradual Progress)*, which I always find soothing. The image is of a tree growing on a mountain against the buffeting of the winds. It kinda forgave me in a way, because at least I'd stood up there and sung the song so I'd made some advance. Sooner or later I was going to have to go out there and face the world.

"Ah Felicity," said Rose as I entered the Post Office. "That was quite some song you sung at the ball."

I was a bit taken aback. Only establishment figures call me by my proper name and it's always intimidating. As for Rose, well she's never called me by any name before. I mumbled something, handed over my bankbook and asked if there was any mail for me.

"What's that name they all call you?" she asked as she searched the pigeonholes that held the mail. "Mouse, is it? How'd you ever end up with a name like that?"

"Just 'cause when I was a kid I was always hiding in corners and that's just what they called me. And Eddie, well, you know, his family are old friends. That's what he's always called me so that's what he introduced me as. I never use my proper name."

"Hmm, no, no mail for you this time." Her eyes are the brown of a bush-shaded creek. For a moment I drowned in them but then she took my bankbook and turned away to call through to the bank.

Down on the beach the tide's rising. The children throw sticks into the waves and see which will wash in first. Lilith gambols in the waves, grabbing at the sticks. She grabs Janey's and tears up the beach with it. Janey runs after her, laughing.

I draw some oxygen into my lungs and turn to Kate.

"You know what, Kate," I say, airily, as if it really is of no great concern. "I want to be called by my real name from now on. 'Mouse' is just a name I was called when I was a kid and there comes a time when you have to move on from kid things. It's Felicity," I offer tentatively.

"Felicity," she repeated. "Well, that's certainly more uplifting than Mouse. You want to come up to Wairua with us this afternoon Felicity? Pete's taking the Beast Machine so there'll be plenty of room."